VOICES OF THE LOST YEAR
A 2020 Anthology of Teen Voices

Edited by
Amber Bliss

Cover Design by
Rashaa Al-Sasah

2020

VOICES OF THE LOST YEAR
A 2020 Anthology of Teen Voices
Edited by Amber Bliss

Copyright © 2020 West Warwick Public Library
All Rights Reserved

All rights reserved. No part of this publication may be reproduced or transmitted in any form or by any means without the prior written permission of the publisher. All characters in this publication are fictitious, and all places in this novel are used fictitiously. Any resemblance to real persons, living or dead, is purely coincidental.

West Warwick Public Library
1043 Main Street
West Warwick, RI 02893
www.wwpl.org

This project was made possible in part by a grant from the RI Office of Library and Information Services using funds from the Institute of Museum and Library Services, and by a generous donation from the Friends of the West Warwick Public Library.

Acknowledgements

We want to thank our incredible guest authors and professionals; Mark Oshiro, Dr. Darcy Little Badger, Linda Addison, Jennifer Dugan, and Carlisle Webber who generously provided their time, wisdom, and experience to our young writers during the summer writing workshop, and we want to thank the staff at the West Warwick Public Library who contributed their efforts to the production and support of this anthology. Writing is often a solitary pursuit but making writing the best it can be takes a village.

Contents

Introduction... 1

Horror

Flash Fiction: The Seamstress; Safe; Perfect Daughter

~Kaia Dahlin... 3

Three young women in this series of short tales explore the darker side of fiction with tales of trauma, revenge from beyond the grave, and an artist's perspective on justice.

Flash Fiction: Necessary; Paranoia; Revenge

~Toshiro Brooks... 14

Peel back the layers of a troubled man's grim history in three sordid tales of misfortune.

Chrysalis

~Theresa Katin.. 22

To bring back the dead, a man and his daughter travel deep into the forest and traffic with an ancient power, but all magic has a price.

The Cost of Help

~Nathan Moone.. 36

After the death of his mother, a young man travels to the South to meet his estranged father and discovers that the masked Hollows aren't the only creatures who aren't what they appear.

Fantasy

The Wolf Crown
~Kerith Fontenault... 58
> *The prince of a foundering Kingdom must confront the truth about his father's legacy and reconcile the grief in his heart, or his humanity won't be the only thing that goes to the wolves.*

In the Coming Tides
~Brianna Timpson... 75
> *Determined to save her people from an ages-old feud, a young mermaid braves the land to break an ancient curse, but her budding friendship with a human girl gives her more to lose than she ever imagined.*

Science Fiction

Fading Orange
~Linden Philo... 95
> *Eighteen-year-old Charlie is grieving the loss of her friend when the time comes to make her choice. Will she conform and continue to live in the engineered paradise of Deali or choose individuality in a frightening otherworld? The Effect Cube waits for no one.*

Contemporary

Justice
~Ali Bryant... 112
> *Confronted with a corrupt school administration, one survivor decides she will not be silenced. It's time to take the fight all the way to the top.*

Introduction

2020 has been a year of unprecedented change and challenges, not the least of which have impacted the youth. With canceled proms, sporting events, limited gatherings, and school closures, many of the common experiences shared by young people has skipped 2020, leaving it a lost year.

But if there is anything I've learned working with communities as librarian, it's that young people are resilient, passionate, and tenacious. The teens I've had the honor of working with on this unique project have continually impressed and inspired me with their creativity and commitment to their craft, and I dare say I've learned as much from them as they did from me while working on this project.

Voices of the Lost Year represents an innovative project that used a grant from the RI Office of Library and Information Services to fund an eleven week writing workshop for Rhode Island teens which culminated in this anthology of their work. Every author in this volume chose to spend their summer writing under a rigorous professional workshop model. They learned from industry professionals, drafted their work from a blank page, and committed to several rounds of demanding editing that would have challenged even experienced authors. The final result is a collection of stories that span an array of genres, interests, and personal truths. These diverse young authors were willing to write their way through a gauntlet during a pandemic to bring their stories into print and make them available to the public.

From technologically advanced utopias to shocking transformations, there's something for everyone in this volume, but beneath the masks, sharp teeth, and magic there's also truth. You'll find truths about prejudice, justice, grief, and regret. You'll also find hope, friendship, and love. School may be out in 2020, but I implore you, dear reader, to spend some time with these young authors. I think you'll find they have something to teach you.

~AMBER BLISS
August 2020

The Seamstress

by
Kaia Dahlin

There is a lot of ugly in this world, but she tries to make it better, one jacket at a time.

The storefront was closed, but the light was still on, and the hum of the sewing machine filled the room. Lizzie reached behind her head and wrapped her hair into a messy bun to get it out of her face. She swayed along to the music from the speaker as she sewed the pieces together and removed the pins as she went. Once the outer pieces were complete, she swept the floor, locked up, and went home.

The next day she opened up the shop, and chose her lining fabric before any customers came in. It had a simple black and white rose pattern with a few red splatters. There was an hour and a half before her first appointment. She ironed the fabric and cut out the pieces, then stitched and serged the edges. Finally, she grabbed a zipper from the bin and sat back down. The door opened and her co-worker strolled in.

"Hey, Dani," she muttered without looking up.

"Have you been here all night?"

"No. I got like three hours of sleep when I got home." She pinned the outer and lining fabrics together and positioned the zipper between them.

"How long until your client comes?"

"Ten minutes, I think."

"Okay, do you want me to help with your belt so you can finish your jacket before they get here?"

"Yeah, that'd be great. Thank you."

Dani walked over to the cabinet, her sneakers squeaking as she went, and grabbed the box of grommets. She placed the box on her table and focused on her task. She finished the belt in five minutes and threaded it through the belt loops. Lizzie put the jacket on one of the store's dress forms, so she could see the final product. Her self-sourced, tanned, and dyed red leather made into a pattern that took her four months to develop.

The bell rang, and she walked to the front of the store to greet the customer. His dark hair drenched with product looked like he dipped it in oil. He had bushy eyebrows above his light blue eyes.

"Hello, are you Xavier Everett?"

"Yes, I am."

"Follow me to the back, please."

They went past the empty worktables and past the fabric bolts until they reached her station. She asked him to extend his arms so she could take the measurements.

"Do you like what you're feeling?"

She scoffed. "Don't flatter yourself. I'm not interested."

"You're not one of *those* are you? Maybe you just haven't met the right guy."

Dani forced herself to not laugh as she went to help another client.

"Yeah, maybe that's it." Lizzie rolled her eyes but saw an opportunity. "Here's my address. Come by tonight."

Xavier left with a smile, thinking he had another score, and they carried on with the appointments. They finished up their day and locked up together so they could go home.

Only Lizzie knows what happened to their missing clients. She can still remember the screams and the looks of terror in their eyes. The same looks and screams that came from their victims.

There is a lot of ugly in the world, but she tries to make it better, one jacket at a time.

Safe

by
Kaia Dahlin

"Could you tell us what happened that day?"

"I'm sorry, what?" I picked at the sleeve of my sweatshirt. My mom grabbed my hand.

It was still stained after ten washes.

"Could you tell me what happened on the afternoon of the 15th?"

"Well, I—it was the day of the school's first Girl's STEM Club Meeting. I had a flannel on because I got dress coded by my video production teacher. I was waiting for the bell to ring and my teacher was telling us about our upcoming project."

"What happened after the bell rang?" His voice sounded like gravel.

"Um… I went to my locker because I was meeting my friend Chloe there. I had to wait like five minutes because her German teacher held the class for a bit. As we walked towards the science lab, I felt like I was being watched. She told me to just brush that feeling away because there were still a lot of people in the halls."

Don't be crazy. The hallway is just crowded. We're safe.

If only you had taken it seriously.

"When we got to the lab, Ms. Wilson told us to put our backpacks outside of the room. I pocketed my phone and swiss army knife and went in. I know it wasn't allowed, but a girl was almost kidnapped three weeks before. We were

6

still on edge. Ms. Wilson had snacks set up on the center table, and she let us go get our homework to keep us busy before the meeting started. After the buses left, the rest of the girls walked in the room."

"Is it possible for you to tell me their names?" He tried to make his voice gentler.

I started picking at the sweatshirt again.

"Do you want to take a break?"

I nodded. My eyes filled with tears as he left the room. He came back with a granola bar and my mom let me lay my head on her shoulder as I ate. She stroked my hair and after I stopped sobbing and she looked me in the eyes.

"You got this, Naomi. You can do it." She was being as calming as she could be while she was also crying.

She always said that to me before I left for school if I had a test that day. *You got this, Naomi. You can do it.* She probably never thought she would say it to me in a police station.

"Are you able to continue?"

"Yeah, yeah. I'm good."

"Can you tell me the girls' names?"

"There was me, Chloe, Gemma, Erika, Ella, Sarah, and Ava."

Two alive. Four dead. One missing. Where are you?

"What happened next?"

"After everyone was there and we did introductions, Ms. Wilson did a run-down of what we were gonna do that meeting. We were gonna make magnetic slime. We got into pairs and chose a lab table. As we gathered the materials for the activity, she realized she forgot the spoons. We were walking to the cafeteria to get spoons before the lunch lady left when he showed up."

"What did he look like?"

"He had pale-ish skin, light blue eyes, and a small scar on his forehead. He was about your height and age."

"What did he do?"

"He followed us. He kept pace. Ms. Wilson confronted him. She told him that he needed to leave if he wasn't faculty. He just took out a knife and kept stabbing her. We ran, screaming in case anyone could hear us. The closest room was the library, so we ran there. He grabbed Ella before she could get inside. Her blood pooled in front of the door. I took my knife out and opened the biggest blade. Chloe told the others to hide as we watched the door. We heard screaming. There was another door..."

There was another door.

"Erika ran to us dragging Gemma behind her. Gemma was bleeding. There was a lot of blood. I took my flannel off and tied it around her side to try and stop the bleeding. I told them to go to the girls' bathroom and hide in the third stall."

"Why the third stall?"

"After the attempted kidnapping, some of the girls decided to hide sharp things in the stall. It's also just the least disgusting stall."

"Why didn't you and Chloe go with them?"

"We knew if we all went, he would follow us and we would all die. Chloe and I knew we had to fight him. We had to fight so at least we had a chance. She ran over to the librarian's desk and grabbed her scissors while I snuck behind the shelves. He was getting closer to her, so I grabbed a dictionary and chucked it at him. It knocked the knife out of his hand, and I ran over and grabbed it. He charged at me, so I ran away."

My heart drummed with the beat of my words like the soundtrack of a movie I watched, but not one I was a part of.

"He caught up and pushed me into a bookshelf. He grabbed his knife back, and I dodged his first attempt. I stabbed his side and I saw him smile. He moved quicker and more aggressively. It was like the blood motivated him. I couldn't breathe. I landed a few more stabs as he punched me. He sliced my thigh and I couldn't stand anymore. I was too tired. Chloe popped out of nowhere and slammed a book over his head. He tripped on a chair leg and hit his head on a table, and he was out. She stabbed him with the scissors and tied her sweatshirt around my thigh. She told me to leave her and go to Erika. That's the last time I saw her."

The last time I saw you. Where are you? Are you okay?

"As I limped to the bathroom, I saw Gemma lying in a pool of blood. After I got to the stall, I tried to comfort Erika as I called the cops. The dispatcher said it would be about ten minutes."

Ten. Stay on the line. Eight. Just breathe. Five. It's okay. Be brave. Three. They're almost there, just hang in there. One. They're close. Can you hear the sirens?

"Thank you. I promise I will do my best to catch this man. You're safe now."

"If I stayed with her, would she still be here?"

"It's hard to say, but you got Erika to safety. That's something to be proud of."

We left the station and drove home. When we pulled into the parking spot, I ran up the stairs to our apartment and went to my room. I flopped down on my bed and felt

9

something under my pillow. A tape recorder with Chloe's bracelet wrapped around it. I pressed play and her voice came out of it.

"I'm so sorry. Please know this isn't your fault." She started crying. "I love you, my dude. Goodbye." A gunshot ended the tape.

She's gone.

Perfect Daughter

by
Kaia Dahlin

It's been one week since my family moved across the country. My parents are at their office holiday party. I didn't go because I still have boxes to unpack and pictures to hang up.

"Eleanor."

My parents aren't supposed to be back for another hour, so it can't be them, and we live miles away from town in the old house everyone avoids as much as they can. I could investigate the noise but would rather stay in my room. I'm probably just imagining things. I put some of my trophies on a shelf that was built into the wall by my closet. A scratching sound came closer and closer but went silent right outside my door.

"Eleanor, I know you're in there," a sing-song voice said.

I shut my eyes and a wave of anxiety crashed over me. I had a baseball bat packed away with some books. I opened the box and grabbed the cold metal, then pushed a box of clothes in front of the door to try and keep it out. It scratched my door, harder than it scratched the walls.

"Who's there?" My voice was shaky.

"You don't recognize my voice, Ellie?"

No, tha—that's impossible. Only one person has ever called me Ellie. The door burst open, crushing the box. I know its face. Her dark hair had started to grow back. The scar from a failed eyebrow slit attempt. It's the face of Evelyn, my sister. My sister who's been dead for one year.

"How are you here? I saw you get buried."

"You don't know how I died, do you?"

"You couldn't handle the constant checkups, so you killed yourself."

She chuckled.

"Well, what actually happened?"

"It was time for dad to drop me off at my appointment. He started the car up to air out the usual coffee stench. I sat on the garage steps and debated which playlist to put on. Mom came into the garage to get dad to take the trash out. He said he would be back soon, but it wasn't true. They just wanted to get rid of me. They had gotten fed up with caring for me and paying my medical bills. They only wanted to care for you, their perfect daughter."

"What's that supposed to mean?"

"Please, like you don't know what that means. They've always cared about appearance and accomplishments. You were captain of your baseball team and everybody knew who you were. I was just Eleanor's sister with cancer. That's all I was. I was mom and dad's way to get pity, and they figured that they would get more if I was dead. They locked the garage door and went next door to wait it out. When I woke up, I could see mom and dad hovering over my lifeless body in a puddle of vomit while dad put the car keys in my hand. They had already made up a story of how I was suicidal and fed it to the entire neighborhood. Everyone believed it, even you."

"They'll be back in an hour."

"They never left the garage."

12

I have to check, even if it's too late. They are the only family I have left. I run down the staircase, through the living room, and push open the garage door. Their car is still there. They're still in their seats, but they're not alive. Mom's makeup is smeared from crying, and their fingers are bloodied. The door slammed behind me and the car turned on. I tried opening the door but it didn't budge. A chuckle came from the other side.

"Evelyn. Evelyn, please. Please stop it."

"Why should I?"

"Evelyn, I—" My vision blurs.

"Sweet dreams, Eleanor."

Necessary

by
Toshiro Brooks

The most important thing you need to understand is that I only did what I did because I thought it was necessary. I thought that the ends would justify the means. Although, if you think it's helped me sleep at night, you don't know the first thing about human nature. Then again, I suppose I'm not exactly an expert on that either.

So, it was necessary. That's what I told myself as I dragged a bag of human remains down an alleyway to the dumpster. That's what I told myself after realizing that there was probably a less painful, and almost certainly less personal way to kill someone than stabbing them. But there was no undoing it, no way of going back and doing things differently.

Once everything was cleaned up, I just had to make a call, get what I wanted, and forget all of this. I was about to do just that when I realized I had misplaced the note I had been given—the one with the number on it.

Now I did eventually find it, on the ground next to the dumpster. But you can bet when I first realized it was gone, I lost my shit. Honestly, can you imagine doing all that and then not getting what you wanted in return? What a waste! I dialed the number.

"Hey, it's me. I did what you asked, now hold up your end of the deal."

"Excuse me?" a confused woman's voice on the other end answered back.

"It's me, I did what you asked."

"Who are you?"

"It's me, *Josh.*"

"I'm sorry, I think you have the wrong number." She hung up.

I called again several times hoping I had just dialed wrong. I slowly and carefully pressed each digit of the number, each time getting the same woman who I had never met before, and who was at this point very suspicious.

So that's it. It was all for nothing. They didn't give me their actual number. And I killed a guy for no reason. I might as well clarify that's the story, but it's not like it makes any difference legally. I'm still a murderer, albeit a murderer who was tricked, who really isn't a very bad person, and who just really, really needed the money.

Paranoia

by
Toshiro Brooks

The trees sway with the breeze. It's overcast and had just started to rain. I can probably make it back before it starts pouring if I'm quick. The street is so quiet, so empty, and yet I feel as if I'm being watched. I've accepted by now that it probably doesn't mean anything, that I'm probably all alone on this quiet little suburban street, but somehow I'm not relieved. Acceptance doesn't lessen the feeling of dread, the need to look over my shoulder every ten seconds.

Was that a man behind that bush, watching me with a sick grin on his face?

No, just my own reflection in someone's window.

Was that the sound of a second set of footfalls, just a tenth of a second behind my own?

No, just the echo of my own steps.

I had gotten better at finding explanations for things, but they never quite comforted me. The feeling will never be gone, the feeling that what happened last time could happen again. That it *would* happen again.

My house is only a few blocks away now. Why had I even left? I told myself it was to get some sun, and yet it had been overcast all day. I hardly ever feel safe in my own house, but I certainly don't feel safe out here on this street, where it's as cold and as quiet as a tomb.

What's that sound? Those footsteps? Are they really just an echo?

Of course they are. Sure, they don't fall in time with my own footsteps, but perhaps that's some sort of auditory distortion due to the rain. Of course, I know that's not how sound works, but I'll dismiss it nonetheless.

I glance back again. I can't help it. I tell myself there's nothing there, and yet in the back of my mind I can already picture the figure following me; some tall, stereotypical "stalker" type in a trench coat and hat. I can't help but think back to a news story I had read about a knife-wielding attacker roaming the streets in a suburban neighborhood. This is how my mind works. I read about something online and it's all I can think about. It keeps me up at night.

The footsteps are growing louder, and I walk faster but the echo keeps pace. My stalker is coming closer, opening his switchblade in preparation to slice my jugular. My therapist tells me I catastrophize. She's right, it really is ridiculous, the thought that of all the people on this planet, this would be happening to me, again.

What are the chances of lightning striking the same person twice? she'd once said. I was tempted to inform her there was a park ranger who'd been struck by lightning seven separate times, and lightning isn't even evil.

I can see my house. It's all I can do not to run as those footsteps follow, keeping pace like a metronome or a ticking clock. I glance back and forth, sure this stalker is real. I'm in danger. If I do see him, what will I do then? Just because I'm looking at him doesn't mean he can't kill me. It's the same mentality as a child thinking the monsters can't get them if they keep the lights on. But that only works if the monsters aren't real. Sometimes they are.

No, I shouldn't think like that. I shouldn't make things worse.

I reach the front door. I slide the key in the lock, glancing back one final time.

My heart skips a beat.

There he is, a man in a trench coat standing across the street, his face hidden by the shadow of a tree. It isn't real. There is no possible way that he is really there. Yet he is. I'm not in great shape, mentally—or physically to be honest—but I'm not prone to hallucinations. If I'm looking at something, it's there.

I stand there staring at this figure for god knows how long, expecting him to either move or turn away, expecting any confirmation that he either was or wasn't a psycho serial killer about to cut my head off. But he doesn't move.

I suppose there's a chance it has nothing to do with me, that he's just someone waiting for a friend or an Uber. But I still run into the house and slam the door with the urgency of someone being chased by a demon. I rush to the window and look back, not wanting to lose sight of the man across the street.

Too late. He's already gone.

And I hear my door creaking open.

Revenge

by
Toshiro Books

The only light source in the room is the window, although it's covered by the blinds. I can see a dresser to one side of me, a twin-size bed on the other. The only other furniture is the chair I've been duct taped to. I've seen YouTube videos on how to escape from duct tape, but the amount of tape wrapped around this chair is so absurd it seems insane to try getting out without some kind of tool.

As I'm awkwardly struggling, I hear someone moving around just outside the door.

After a minute, presumably spent relishing my attempts to escape, my captor pushes open the door.

The guy has a real smug smile, like he thinks it's absolutely hilarious that he kidnapped me.

"Heya. Man, you've seen better days. Not taking things well, are you?"

"Do I know you or something?"

"Oh, right…" he says, flicking on the light. "Recognize me?"

It takes my eyes a second to adjust before I see him clearly. And I have no idea who the hell he is.

"No. I've never met you in my life."

"Heh, you don't even remember me. Why am I not surprised?"

I'm trying to keep my composure, but I'm scared. There isn't really anything threatening about him, he's just a guy.

But as you can imagine it doesn't really matter who they are; if someone has you taped to a chair in one of their spare rooms, you're scared of them.

"Look, I don't know you."

"But I know you. I know who you are."

"I didn't do anything to you."

"Do you think I'm stupid?"

I decide not to answer that question, considering angering him isn't the safest idea right now. I don't know what this guy is capable of, but if he thought I would recognize him it makes me think he isn't worried about the possibility of me escaping.

"Of course you think I'm stupid, that's a given," he says, throwing his arms up in the air. "I had plans, I had things to do, but I canceled them, because I thought of something more fun to do with my day." He leaned forward, his smile growing wider. "Revenge."

I'm wracking my brain, trying to find an escape route. Then it hits me—the chair. If I can break the chair, I can get the duct tape off. But I need to wait until this lunatic leaves the room.

"What to do now? I have you at my mercy, I could literally kill you at any moment. And until then, I can savor the look of pure fear in your eyes."

His doorbell rings. Perfect.

"Damnit, I told you not to come over today," he says under his breath as he walks out.

I lean forward, and I'm able to get myself into a standing position. I run backwards at the wall, throwing all my weight against it, and the chair breaks with a loud crack. The back snaps off and the rest of it hits the floor with a crash.

Although he has to be aware that I'm escaping, at least it'll take him a moment to get the person at his door away. I peel the duct tape off myself, but I have no plan for where to go next. What if this guy lives on the third story of an apartment building? I rush to the window and look out. To my relief the ground is only a few feet away. I'm on the first floor.

I hear the door swing open, and I smash the window with a piece of the chair. I climb out as fast as I can and tumble to the ground. But now I'm out, in broad daylight. I run like hell.

I have no idea who the guy was or why he went to the trouble of kidnapping me, which isn't exactly comforting. But now I'm out. Hopefully I won't see him again.

Hopefully.

Chrysalis

by
Theresa Katin

"When can we go home?"

She asked the question more times than he could count. Each time, he could tell her impatience was growing. He wanted to go home too, home to their snug cottage on a cliff where you could hear the roar of the waves and taste the salt in the air. A multitude of flowers bloomed in a tiny garden in front of their house, the house with buttery yellow paint, chipped ever so slightly. Chipping away, like her patience. Like his sanity.

"Dad?"

"Look." He pointed to the space between two trees.

"What?" Lucy glanced around as a smile crept onto her face.

"I saw something over there."

"Something bad?"

"No, something good."

A bright orange butterfly drifted down towards them. It wasn't a monarch; instead of black dots and lines it had golden yellow tips. Sunlight bounced off its wings and made the butterfly glow.

Moira... The vibrant color was similar to his wife's red hair.

The butterfly glided over to Lucy and batted her nose. "It likes me!" she giggled.

I miss her so much.

Jacob and Lucy continued down the dirt path, deeper into the forest.

"Wasn't that fun, Dad?" Lucy patted the leather satchel that hung from his shoulder.

"It was."

"When I grow up, I'm gonna live with butterflies. Loads of 'em. I'll have a house and backyard full of butterflies that are all different colors." She skipped alongside her father and hummed to herself, no doubt imagining her future home.

"Mm-hmm. Sure, honey."

They came upon a massive tree covered with orange butterflies. Cantaloupe, marigold, and tangerine all stirred once they noticed the people strolling in their direction. A few left their perches and descended toward Lucy and Jacob.

Lucy gasped and her face lit up. "Dad, look! Look at them."

He stared at them for a few moments, amazed at the abundance of color, then glanced down at Lucy and smiled. Jacob was so happy that the little winged creatures delighted her. It pained him to say, "Lucy, we have to keep going."

She frowned and crossed her arms. "Aw, Dad, really?"

"Yes. You know that, come on." He grabbed her hand and she reluctantly followed him.

If we stop, we'll never make it in time. This needs to be done. I have to fix this.

Those orange butterflies had brought such joy to Lucy, but they bothered him.

Jacob strode ahead and glanced back the way they came to check on his daughter. She had pulled free from his grip and wandered behind him, waving flowers and singing to herself.

23

He was about to turn back around and continue forward when something caught his eye: a few psychedelic specks floating in the distance. He stopped to look more closely.

They were orange butterflies, following them along the path. Despite their warm hue, a chill seeped into his bones.

"Lucy."

She stopped singing and stared at the butterflies, transfixed. Her little bouquet lay neglected on the forest floor.

"Lucy."

This time she turned to face him.

"Why are they following us?"

"I don't know. Come on, honey, we have to keep going."

* * *

The more time they spent in the woods, the more awake it seemed. As Jacob and Lucy hiked farther and farther, the trees around them grew so dense Jacob couldn't walk along the path without a branch brushing against his arm. He'd been hit in the head by a tree branch after getting distracted more than once.

It's my responsibility to make things right.

"Dad?"

"What, Lucy?" He couldn't keep the fatigue out of his voice. "Don't ask to stop because you know we—"

"No, Dad, look at the tree. Is that…"

She didn't have to finish her sentence. In front of them was a tree coated in a crimson substance that looked like blood.

"Oh my god," he whispered.

That's crazy. It's not blood. We're in the middle of a goddamn forest.

"It's not blood." He wasn't completely certain, but for Lucy's sake he shook the exhaustion from his voice.

"Are you sure?"

Jacob searched for a response. "Yes, I'm sure. Trust me."

The alarming sight made something click in his brain. The vermilion things on the tree were red butterflies coated in blood.

I was out with Lucy when they broke in. I should have been there. She shouldn't have been alone.

Butterflies erupted from the tree and dove straight at them. Lucy shrieked as Jacob pulled her tight and ran. Ruby droplets rained down on them and pelted his back and head. Warmth oozed through his clothes and trickled down his spine. He choked as it entered his mouth. Copper tainted the air and nausea rippled through him as paper-thin wings sliced his skin.

He had no idea how long he ran. Some time ago they veered off the path and managed to escape. He reached up to wipe the sweat from his forehead, and his hand returned slick and scarlet. Between the killer insects and thorn-riddled brush, he couldn't tell what blood was from the butterflies and what was his own.

At least we'll have enough.

Lucy hadn't said anything since the attack. Instead, she clung to his leg and whimpered softly. She wasn't hurt too badly. Physically, at least. Most of the cuts were on Jacob. The dried blood clotting in her hair was from the butterflies.

Jacob stopped for a moment to open his blood-splattered satchel. Inside was a brown notebook that held directions. After reading a page, he put it back and zipped up his bag. He gazed at the sun setting between the trees, casting a golden glow over the flora and fauna. It looked so peaceful, but he wasn't fooled.

"Come on, this way." He turned and started walking towards a large pine, and past it, a clearing. "We're almost there."

"Where? Where are we going?"

Jacob didn't reply.

"And why is it getting so dark? I'm tired, Dad. I want to sleep," she whined.

"We can't rest, honey. We have to keep going." She was on the verge of having a meltdown, and if that happened, he knew they weren't moving until morning. But they needed to get there that night.

He scooped her up in his arms and carried her over to the glade.

"Why? Please tell me." She paused. "Is it 'cause of Mom? The butterflies remind me of her, too."

He didn't respond.

* * *

They arrived at the clearing, a circle of dirt surrounded by lush emerald grass. It felt tucked away, hidden within the layers of the forest. The light faded even faster. They were almost out of time.

Jacob set Lucy down on the grass at the outskirts of the circle, removed the leather bag from his shoulder, and swung

26

it onto the ground. After rummaging through it for a few moments, he pulled out a plastic bag of purple berries, two black candles, one white candle, and a pack of matches. He reached into the bag for his pocketknife but decided against it.

We won't need more.

He walked along the edge of the tree line, checking the base of each trunk. They were supposed to leave it in one of these.

Jacob crouched down and opened a secret door that blended in with the tree's rough bark. Inside was a short wooden stick that at first glance seemed gnarled and ancient but was actually engraved with markings and symbols.

He brought it back to where his backpack sat.

"What is that?"

"A special stick," he said.

"What is it for?"

"To draw things in the dirt."

"What things?"

"Guidelines."

Lucy sat back in the greenery, watching her father's every move. He knew she wouldn't understand, not now, and maybe not for a long time, but that didn't matter. The only thing important now was making sure it worked.

Jacob's gaze landed on the bag of berries. "Here," he said, taking three and holding them out to her. "Eat these."

"What are they?"

"They'll help you sleep." His stomach twisted. "Just eat them."

"Sleep? Why—" But she had already popped the berries into her mouth, lips stained purple as she drifted off mid-sentence.

Jacob approached the patch of dirt and made a couple marks with the stick. He gently picked up Lucy and set her down on her back in the middle of the circle. She looked so helpless, lying down with her hair spread around her like a halo.

That's how I found Moira. Lying in a pool of blood, all alone. Helpless. Her eyes were open, but she was gone.

The white candle went six inches above Lucy's head, the two black candles six inches from either side of her face. After a few attempts he struck a match and lit each candle, starting with the two black ones and ending with the white. Slowly, he drew one final symbol and stepped away to his satchel. He opened a small brown book to check his notes, then took a silver dish and placed it at her feet. He referenced the book one last time, then began to speak.

"Two candles for death, one for life, release us from unending strife. Take this blood, liquid strength divine, return the power to what once was mine. Give back her mind, her spirit; make her whole. Give back her form of flesh and bone."

He gazed down at Lucy, faltering, and prayed her eyes would stay shut.

Jacob spoke again in a different language, so ancient it was all but forgotten. He repeated the chant, voice louder with every line.

"With the help of Mother Nature's might, return her to us by midnight. See this child, afraid and alone, let her warmth call her mother home."

28

Again, he spoke in that primordial tongue, drawing upon the power of beings who came long before him. A voice whispered inside his head:

We are not ones to ignore; we know how to kill and summon storms. Beware my temper and crown of thorns. Do not fail; you have been warned.

The red streaks clinging to Lucy liquefied and shifted upwards. The silky strands moved through the air and pooled in the silver bowl. Still chanting, Jacob rushed over to one of the black candles and let three drops of hot wax fall into the dish. He placed it back in the dirt, then grabbed the other black candle and did the same. Finally, he took the white candle and held it over the dish so that seven drops of wax fell in. Jacob returned the candle to its place near Lucy's head.

The dwindling sunshine glimmered out of the corner of his eye, as if the sun had allowed its fingers to slip through the trees and let go. Clouds darkened as the minutes passed, and soon the only light was from the flickering candles. Shadows swelled and danced across the trunks of evergreens.

The blood mixture in the bowl started churning, stirred by an invisible hand, and drained from the bowl while the candle flushed pink, then darker. The dish was empty in moments, gleaming silver, and the candle had become a deep burgundy.

"Two candles for death, one for life, release us from unending strife. Take this blood, liquid strength divine, return the power to what once was mine. Give back her mind, her spirit; make her whole. Give back her form of flesh and bone. With the help of Mother Nature's might, return her to us by midnight. *See this child, afraid and alone, let her warmth call her mother home."*

Jacob shuddered. During the last line his voice merged with the one in his head.

The wind picked up, rattling branches and sending leaves flying. The sky swirled like a boiling cauldron. Grays, blues, and purples mushed together, watercolor bruises up above. Trees groaned and leaned in toward the glade, eager to glimpse the disaster unfolding.

Lucy writhed on the ground. Her eyes were still shut, but she twisted, and her face contorted in pain.

No, no, no. They said this could happen. But the berries should have worked, she shouldn't be able to wake up yet.

He ran over to his bag and tore through his notebook, furiously turning page after page. *Those hideous witches said she'd be fine. The berries were supposed to put her to sleep for three hours, that way there was no chance she'd wake in the middle.*

One of the black candles went out and Lucy screamed.

He rushed over and frantically tried to light it, but the match kept slipping from his hands. *No, no. God no. I can't lose her too.* Eventually the wick caught flame; whether it was Fate throwing him a bone or if it was by chance, he didn't care. It didn't explain what was wrong with Lucy.

The glint of a granola bar wrapper stuck out of her skirt pocket. His heart dropped.

Days before, he trekked through the forest to find the witch's moss-covered hovel shrouded in vines and mystery. They were grotesque and clever beings, not vain or obsessive like they were so often portrayed. Bile crept up his throat as he shuffled into their woodland hut. On that day he met with one who spoke for herself and the rest. She was their leader, of sorts. Apparently, they could take many forms; this was just easier for him to comprehend.

When the berries were brought up, she said, *Never more than three, unless you want her to sleep forever. And the girl must eat them on an empty stomach.*

Jacob held his head in his hands. *There was a rule. Of course, there was a rule. Shit. How could I forget? She must have snuck the granola bar out of my bag when I wasn't looking. How could I be so careless?*

All three candles extinguished at once. Lucy was motionless on the ground while tears streamed down her face. A bitter wind ripped through the clearing and knocked over the silver dish.

"No, no, no," he muttered. Jacob cautiously stepped onto the symbols in the dirt, and when nothing happened, he dashed to her side. "I'm sorry. I'm so sorry. It should have worked, something went wrong, I—"

For a brief moment he saw his wife's face in the lingering smoke, frozen in the cool night air. Then it vanished. This had all been for nothing. Sobs racked his body as he sat on the ground staring at his daughter. *I'm so sorry, darling. It wasn't supposed to happen like this.*

Those vile, god-awful witches. It's their ridiculous spell that didn't work. This is all their fault. He stood up, marched across the clearing towards the eldritch stick and snapped it in half. Still not satisfied, he chucked one part into the forest, turned around and threw the other half in the opposite direction.

31

We should never have come here. I should never have believed those loathsome, two-faced liars. Oh god, what would Moira think?

Jacob collected the candles and his book and shoved them in his bag. He flung it over his shoulder and tenderly picked up Lucy. He scuffed out the symbols for good measure so it wouldn't look like a summoning circle.

How could I have been so foolish? He shook his head. *Of course it didn't work. It never would have worked. I can't do magic. I'm just another moron pining after the impossible. Moira, I'm so sorry.* Lucy stirred as he started down the path, flashlight in hand.

"Dad?" She rubbed her eyes.

"You're awake."

"Were you crying?"

"No," he said quickly.

"Are we going home now?"

He sighed. "Yes."

She shifted around to look over Jacob's shoulder. "Who is that?"

"What?"

"There's someone over there."

"Where?"

Lucy pointed to the glade. He turned around and spotted a figure in the shadows. The clouds parted, giving way to moonlight and he gasped.

His wife.

"It worked," Jacob whispered. He raced toward her.

At the edge of the grass he set Lucy down and made sure she could stand before embracing his wife.

"Oh my god, Moira, it's you! It's really you. I didn't think it would work, but you're here. How are you here?" He clung to her even tighter. "I don't even care how this happened. I'm just so glad you're alive."

"You fool." Moira pushed him away.

Jacob fell and fumbled around trying to find the flashlight. "What? What do you mean?"

"Moira is dead."

"What? But...you're her? Why do you look like her?" The swell of hope in his chest withered and turned to dust.

"Are humans really so naive? You can't bring back the dead."

"Did you think that's what we were doing?" Lucy walked over to the woman and stood by her, staring at Jacob.

"Lucy?"

The witch who looked like Moira spoke. "No, not anymore. By the way, splendid job using her like that. I didn't think you would sacrifice your only daughter in a ritual you knew nothing about to retrieve your dead wife. So desperate. What would she have thought?"

"Yes, bravo. We always did underestimate the humans, Clara. They're constantly exceeding our expectations," Lucy said. A flare of pointed teeth glinted in the dark.

"Indeed. Much more stupid than we could ever imagine."

Jacob's bewilderment turned to anger at their levity. Were they mocking him? "What the hell is going on? What have you done to Lucy?" *My dear, sweet Lucy.*

"You mean, what have you done to Lucy? She's gone. Bringing life to the dead is impossible, but we seized the opportunity to restore one of our own," Clara said.

33

"Abellona was caught in an endless place between the living and the dead."

"A real hellhole," she interjected.

"And now she is reunited with us at last," Clara finished.

"What do you mean, what have I done to Lucy? I did exactly what you told me to. You gave me the tools and I followed your instructions. You said she wouldn't be harmed—"

"And she hasn't been. Not by us. You're the one who did this to her. You're the one who cast her soul into oblivion. The one who freed me. This is all your fault."

Those words were like a knife to the chest. He cowered on the forest floor, dirt and pebbles grinding into his knees. "No. No! She's not—she can't be…."

"She's gone. I'm only holding onto this child's body until I find a suitable replacement. I figured I'd play along for a while, but my sister found us so fast." Abellona knelt and stroked his face. "I am grateful for your help, though, however unwilling it was."

When he swatted her hand away, she stood up and chuckled.

Jacob closed his hand around the light and flashed it in their faces. Clara looked so similar to Moira, but different. She grinned and her teeth shone in the light, sharp just like Abellona's. Her face was sunken and she had dark circles under her eyes. Those eyes…

Jesus Christ.

He looked down at Abellona and her eyes flared in the light, bright yellow.

"Oh my god." He stepped back, scrambling to get away.

34

"He can't help you." Clara laughed, a high-pitched cackle that reverberated through the forest.

"Here," said Abellona. She offered five purple berries in her outstretched hand. "It's still possible for you to see your wife and child."

What choice do I have? They're both dead because of me. I don't deserve to live.

"Well?" she said expectantly. "Make your choice."

His eyes darted from one to the other, wife to child. Jacob swallowed the berries and closed his eyes.

The Cost of Help

by
Nathan Moone

Mother didn't want me with her in those final moments. Crickets beckoned the night sky and a cold breeze siphoned the warmth of her presence. I sat by the well as her coughs grew fainter throughout the night. The doctor kept her company while the damp earth soaked my breeches.

I don't want to curse you along with me, she would wheeze.

She grew frailer with each passing day. My days, however, consisted of nothing but being at her beck and call. Helping her with every little need and action. I slept out in the shed for a while. Lumps grew all over, her skin faded, now a pale torn sheet. Her harsh decline happened in a short time. I soon boxed up her smoking pipe and her slender hands and needles stopped fixing the holes in our clothes. She wasn't as kind as I expected of people, like the characters in my stories, nonetheless, she was the only person I had. I didn't get to go out much.

Mother began coughing again. Thundering cries ripped apart her lungs. I prayed that this would be the last I'd hear of them.

God soon answered.

* * *

I buried her on a Sunday. The doctor left to contact the authorities and make the necessary arrangements. It would take him a half a day's ride to get back to the city. I began digging when the sun came up. Her body was as light as I imagined. The doctor had wrapped her in her bedsheets, for which I was grateful—I didn't want to imagine throwing dirt over her face, though I would be lying if I claimed I didn't feel a sliver of enjoyment at the thought. Even prior to the sickness I would tend to the property or be on my hands and knees in the garden for hours on end. She cooked rarely. Her favorite activity was to point out any flaws left from my back-breaking work. Despite this, each scoop of dirt was harder than the last.

* * *

Only a few days later a man came back to the house. Mother wasn't the biggest fan of visitors. I was kind of glad really. Mother lived a good enough life to make sure that we didn't have to worry about money. That's how she explained it anyway. The visitor showed me on this oppressive day that Mother wasn't only a harsh controlling woman, but also a liar.

To the Son of Madam Brenner,

It is with my deepest sorrow to hear the Former Madam Brenner has passed from this world into the next. It saddens Father to know that you will now be traveling alone in this world without another to look after and care for you in these trying times. However, it is with the sincerest grace that Father extends his request to see you safely back to his land to ensure your further education, career, and familial duties that Mother has stripped from you.

Signed at the behest of Mister Brenner,

Klei.

Not long after, I filled a knapsack with the few books Mother cared to buy for me and what little clothes I possessed. The visitor sat on the driving bench of his carriage by the time I came out of the cabin. I eyed the simple Cross stuck in the ground as I left home behind. She would be overlooking the horizon for the rest of her days. Only one future would greet me if I stayed here. The only difference was there wouldn't be a soul to bury me.

* * *

I know as much about the South as I do about Father— next to nothing. Mother took me North eighteen years ago saying that Father only had one true calling. Not a husband, a father, or a gentleman, but his work. Mother's money wasn't from her own resources at all, in fact, it came from Father.

The roads were rougher than I expected. We camped out most nights in silence—it wasn't until our third night that my sunburned overseer provided me with Hugh as his name. He didn't say much else the duration of the trip.

Hugh and our caramel horse, Luis, were out of sight while I sat in the carriage making for a lonely trip that allowed me to mull over Father's letter multiple times a day. As each day progressed the mornings turned warmer. Hugh still wore his overcoat and pants without complaint, so I didn't complain either. Luis didn't have any bother of course. It wasn't until halfway through our journey that I saw something not even my books described.

The long stretch of path we followed never seemed to end. Each time I peeked in front of us I never saw anything but road to the horizon. A bright pink and orange sky lit the path, and up ahead was what led me to join Hugh on the riding bench for the first time. Shadowy figures walked towards us, too far away for me to pick out details. Hugh reached behind him and untucked a long musket from one of the sacks behind his bench.

"What are those?" Each clop from the horse drew us closer.

"Don' pay them no mind."

Hugh placed the musket in his lap and cracked the reins. The roaring heat spiraled into ice-cold sweat. I watched as the horse picked up the pace. Hugh aimed the rifle towards the dark figures in the distance. As we drew closer to their harsh panting, I noticed more details. They stood on two feet and held a variety of tools in their arms. Shovels, sickles, axes. They all wore dark black outfits with white trim all in various states of dirtiness. Gloves covered their hands to hide their deformed grabbers as only three shapes sprouted from their palms. From a distance, I thought they could have been human. As I looked at their faces fear took over.

Each of them wore a dark wooden mask depicting a boar to cover their heads. Their eyes so deeply hidden in their masks that I could only see a dark red surrounding the black eye holes. Hugh gripped his weapon even tighter as we cantered by them. Two men walked behind the group of six looking equal parts rough as they were intimidating. They held an air around them like cattle dogs herding sheep. Hugh simply nodded at them as we passed.

* * *

Hugh left his musket out for the rest of the ride. I no longer looked forward to my new home with a timid excitement, but rather with a lingering worry that only escalated as we passed more and more of these groups. On the last day, I decided to sit up on the carriage with Hugh so that I could get a lay of the land. We couldn't have asked for a better day. It was Saturday with the sun nice and bright over our heads, luckily not hot enough to be unbearable. It was easy to tell when we were getting close. The rough dirt road turned into a pristine flattened path. Tall oak trees lined the way treating us with a wonderful deep shade. Father's house sat in the distance.

Never in all my years did I even imagine a house so big. I would later be corrected that a manor was the official name. Beautiful white columns lined the front of the building, two stories as windows graced the top floor. I couldn't even comprehend what the inside would look like.

"What happens when we stop?" My eyes beamed as big as they could get trying to soak up every little detail.

"We will be goin' up to Mister Brenner an' he will take you from there."

Hugh slowed the horse down as we drew closer to the home. Short green fields of crop peeked out further behind the house. Little hunched bodies dotted the green. At this rate, I could only guess how many workers Father had on his payroll.

We stopped in front of the house. Hugh dismounted, then walked up to Luis and gently rubbed his muzzle. As I stepped down, the large front doors clicked open. The wide smile I wore vanished as the mask greeted me. I backed up into the cart and banged my head. A dark jaguar stood at the

41

threshold. The mask was the same material as the others we'd passed. As was the outfit. The bright red paint inside the eye holes shucked my soul into the dark pits.

The jaguar stood still with its arms behind its back.

Hugh pulled me from my trance with a hand on my shoulder

He guided me closer to her. "Klei, this is Mister Brenner's son. Do take him as instructed."

We were only a few feet away before he stopped.

"As you wish." Her voice was sweet and feminine. "If you'd please." She turned to the side to allow me room to enter the manor.

I gave one final glance towards Hugh as I walked inside, my feet as heavy as they were.

My shoes clicked underneath an ornate wooden floor, further dressed with a printed carpet covering most of the hall. A tall set of stairs shaped in a curvy L rose to the northeast of me. Beautiful pieces of art covered various spots of the wall as did multiple golden candle fixtures.

Klei moved past me and through the doorway to the left of us. The living room was quite what I expected it to be down to the large fireplace and even nicer sofa, and books lined the walls. I followed a few steps behind her. Just like the others, her gloves only had three fingers.

"So, Klei, what do you do for my father?" Trepidation rattled in my head.

"My duty is to provide him counsel and financial work." She continued into a hallway. Her gait held a curious form rather like a slither on two legs than a bounce.

"So you help run the farm?"

42

Klei spun around fast enough for me to almost crash into her, bringing me face to fang.

"Here is your room, Young One, Father shall be expected soon." She gripped the knob and pushed the door open. "If you would like, you may explore the grounds. Father may take a few hours."

"Thank you, Klei." I paused.

"No thanks, it is my duty."

When I didn't add anything, she walked back the way we came.

"I hope it's not rude of me to ask."

She stopped in her tracks and looked back.

"But why the…" I gestured up at my face.

"You do not have us where you come from, correct?"

"Us?"

She stood a moment longer. Time was still between us.

"Welcome home, Young One."

Without a breath more, she left me alone with more questions than answers.

* * *

By the time I awoke from my nap, I was dry from the bath. Despite several hours passing, the sun was still shining down. I slid out of bed and put some clothes on, then paused, holding my breath to hear if anyone was around. Nothing. I stepped into the hall and looked over my surroundings. Paintings sprouted like flowers, all of which were various nature pieces.

I quickly made my way to the back door of the manor, eager to be back into the bright new world. The workers stood picking away further in the distance.

I may as well walk the grounds.

It took only a few minutes to reach the endless field of tobacco. Much to my surprise, a few buildings stood to the left of me. Small wooden houses framed the outskirts of the property, not at all like the finery of the manor. The hired hands must have a small settlement here as Hugh and I hadn't passed any towns nearby. The closest must have been a two-day ride?

My short walk soon brought me closer to the outbuildings. I yearned to finally see more of what my future would be like here.

The air took a sudden turn. Chills tickled my neck. I was nothing more than a rabbit in the presence of a wolf.

My brisk pace diminished to a halt. Memories slammed into me. The lumps on Mother grew with each passing day. Fat on her body faded to nothing more than a skeleton. I could smell her rotting from the inside out. Why could I smell her here?

Most of the wood on the houses brimmed with rot. There had to be dozens of these shacks, all identical. As I finally reached the short steps in front of me, they felt higher than any tree I've climbed. As my foot settled on the thin plank, I regretted that first step.

Its loud groan smashed the silence into a million little pieces. A small face greeted me at the door. My bones locked up as we stared at one another. Red framed his eyes much like the others. No mask greeted me, only a young boy in the dark. Not even the sun dared to enter his home.

44

"Hello?" I whispered.

"I see you've made yourself comfortable!" A booming voice to my left startled the soul out of me. A man a bit taller than me walked over with a big smile on his face. "I expected you in the manor."

I turned once more to look back at the door only to be met with nothing.

"I—I'm sorry but I take it you're..?" My mind still reeled in every direction but straight.

He placed his large sun-kissed hand heavily on my shoulder. "If you don't get it in one guess, I'll assume you have your mother's wits." He, not so gently, grabbed my shoulder to point me back to the manor.

"Who was that boy in there?"

I went to look back, and he stopped me by putting his arm around my shoulder. I could smell his efforts of the day even more clearly.

"Nothing to concern yourself with."

His simple answer left me with a sick taste in my mouth, but after all that he'd done to bring me here, I only had two options. I certainly did not want to go back home.

* * *

Father and I sat at the oak dining table. Savory scents of food wafted from the kitchen.

"This very table was cut down from the fine grove out front!" Food flew out of his mouth in between his comments and poor jokes.

"Who cut it down?"

He didn't very much appreciate nor respond to my question.

It was when the fourth plate was brought out, I began to object to his more than excessive attempts to impress me. Klei ignored my raised hand as she set the ham down.

"Thank you."

She bowed as she backed away, lowering her carved jaw towards me, then returning to her place at the side of the room.

"You're most welcome." Father's gaze was transfixed on me. "So, you know why I wanted to bring you out here?"

I wiped at my face with the napkin, taking careful precautions about what I should say.

"You wanted me to help you with your farm?"

He sliced the ham in front of him with quick, jerking movements.

"Not entirely." He paused to rip a bite out of the flesh. "Your Mother and I weren' exactly eye to eye on how I made us our fortune. Seeing as she up and left us I figured I could finally get the young man who will carry on the Brenner name!" His voice echoed off the walls.

"I appreciate you bringing me here Sir, I really do, I just can't seem to wrap my head around...everything." I gestured around the room.

He let my response hang in the air as he finished off the last of his meal.

"I know, I know," he said between his final mouthfuls. "You have a lot to learn. I don't expect you to be able to cultivate my tobacco overnight." He snapped his fingers.

Klei walked over and took his empty plate. Father gripped her wrist and she froze. "Nor how to handle the *inner*

46

workings and sacrifices one must make." He winked at her before slapping her on the ass.

I watched without saying a word despite digging my nails into the wooden arms of the chair.

Klei didn't flinch when he let go. She moved on from his plate with crisp efficiency and walked over to mine. Her dark eyes peered down at me. It took a few moments before I could compose a coherent response. I handed her my untouched portion and shakily gripped the sides of the chair.

"Klei," Father's voice rang again. "I better not see that slice where it doesn't belong." She disappeared around the corner. He locked his eyes with me once again. "I don't have enough to go around. It would be unfair if one Hollow had special treatment more than the others. Don't you think?"

"H—hollow?" I coughed to clear my throat and leaned back into the chair to look relaxed.

His eyes bulged out wider and his jaw dropped.

"It seems like Mommy didn't inform you about a lot of things. Then again, I'm sure there weren't any up North." I watched as Father pushed his chair out to stand up. "Hollows are the creatures who wear the masks. Just one look at what's under them can turn any man into a grotesque savage." He motioned for me to stand up and follow him. "They all have special talents of course: the jaguars, like Klei, are best suited for housework. The boars are skilled laborers, birds are best for hunting, the ranking goes on. You'll come to understand them all."

Father guided me through the halls and up the long staircase, Klei's steps clicked behind us at a suitable distance. Noticeably out of eyesight. She stopped far behind us before Father did.

47

"Now, because it's your first day home I'm not gonna go and nitpick. But, one thing needs to be made clear." He stopped at a large set of bright reflective mirrors. Two golden handles were placed at waist height begging to be touched. Father gripped both handles and parted the doors like the seas opening into the rush of unforgiving waves.

Dozens of masks and mirrors lined the walls, all of which were in immaculate order. As we stepped in, he moved towards his desk at the center of the room. A tall stack of papers perched on one corner, otherwise, it was just him and the giant leather chair he plopped himself in.

"In my house and especially out on the grounds never give an inch to anything in a uniform. There are a few other men on hand to guide them and push them into doing as they should, however, you need to make it clear that you won't be walked over."

"You want me to treat them like dogs?" The shock I carried was clearly mistaken.

"Even stricter. Your safety must come first, boy. If you'd seen the things they have done to my less fortunate hands..." He didn't continue.

"These mirrors for instance, with their masks on Hollows can't stand to see themselves. It shows them the true nature of the unnatural beings they are. Any look at themselves and they just freeze. Then they start harming themselves. Disgusting, really."

"If they're so dangerous why do you have them around?" I pried my eyes off his magnetic gaze and took in the details of the wall.

48

"Why do we use bulls?" He finished with a laugh. When he noticed I wasn't laughing, he pressed. "Don't tell me your Mother went and spoiled your mind."

"She had a hard-enough time getting sick. She doesn't deserve that much credit." I turned back to him.

His knuckles turned white.

"If you don't want to be here, it will be just as easy for me to send you back to that rotting lake-view you call home. You better not expect to be receiving those supplies I've been sending either." His face flushed red.

I kept my mouth shut against my urge to yell at him for his disgusting behavior.

"You can either end your day by keeping your mouth shut or by walking out the front door. I have plenty of other bastards to carry on my name."

I turned sharply and left the room.

* * *

The rest of the day was silent. I sat in my room trying to come to terms with the situation. How can I be here and use others like animals? What the hell did he mean they can turn men savage? My thoughts were dizzying.

A few short taps on the door drew my attention.

"Yes?" I stood up from the bed and briskly made my way to the door, not at all excited for another argument. It opened to a surprise.

"Klei?"

"Is there anything I can provide for you tonight?" Her voice was just a pitch above a whisper.

A rag was tied around her arm. Even in the darkness, the red in it was unmistakable.

I surveyed the hall to make sure it was clear before gesturing her to come in. She did without hesitation. As soon as she shut the door, my hands shook. Though I must have had a million questions, I had no clue where to start.

"What happened to you? Did father do this?"

Despite the brashness of my attitude she never changed her posture.

"We are tools. Father uses us as he sees fit."

"Sit down, please." I gently offered her my hand.

She looked down at it for a moment before gently taking hold and letting me guide her to the bed.

"Will you let me take a look?"

"I am okay, Young One, it is just a scratch." She studied me and added, "Though I appreciate your assistance."

I knelt next to her to get a better hold on the makeshift bandage. While I untied the tight knot, a harsh hiss escaped the mask. Three different tears in the arm of her dress bled as I unwrapped the bandage. It looked as if someone scratched at her. The softness of her dark skin hid behind the stickiness of the blood.

"What do you know about healing?" Her discomfort was clear.

"I'm no doctor, though I helped Mother clean her wounds and change her bandages when the tumors broke through her skin."

"Mother was a harsh woman…'

My eyes widened.

"But she didn't deserve that curse."

"You knew my mom?" I grabbed the bucket of clean water used for bathing.

"Only a little. I was made into Father's keep right before the marriage. She adored him. Up until she let one of us go."

"She let one of you go?" I washed her injury gently. "I can't imagine her doing anything like that."

"Father was getting too close to her for Mother's liking. She paid the price in the end. We all do. Especially under Father."

"Father did this to you?"

"What? These? I'd much prefer this over what else is in his power. He doesn't bat an eye at making us sick or causing more permanent damage."

I finished tying off the rag and almost kicked the water bucket next to my foot. Klei wasn't put off by what she was telling me.

"Why?" My voice dropped like a stone.

"Why help me with my wounds?" She stood leaving me alone on the bed.

"I don't know. I didn't think about it. Isn't it just the right thing to do?"

"That's what I thought when I gave my son the leftover food months back." She didn't need to say more about what happened next. "Father is expecting me back soon." She walked to the door without waiting for my input.

"You're just going to go back to him?"

"If I don't the others suffer. I know from experience, Young One."

I jumped up and rushed after her.

"Then let me help you! How can I stop him?"

She placed her hand on the doorknob and paused.

51

"If you want to help me put an end to this. Then come with me now." She opened the door and waited for me to follow. I crossed the threshold and quietly closed the door behind me.

She led the way up the stairs as I followed in her shadow. The grandfather clock ahead of us read ten past twelve, Sunday.

"What are we—"

"Shh!" She raised her disfigured glove for emphasis. We passed Father's study, treading lightly to the last door on the right.

"You go into Father's office and grab the key from the top right drawer. I'll meet you at the steps. I need to get something from his room. I'll show you the truth you seek."

I shook my head and walked back to where my reflection waited. Klei was gone when I looked back up the hall. Ever so slightly, I tried to part the doors. They didn't even budge. I pulled a bit harder until they finally shifted.

CRACK!

I stumbled when the doors swung open and gripped the handle tight on instinct to keep from falling and making even more noise.

Frost spread from head to toe as air trapped itself in my throat. Footsteps beat closer and closer. His breathing grew louder. My head hung low, eyes closed.

How could I explain myself?

Moments passed.

Nothing.

I cracked my eyes open. Still nothing.

My heart stopped thumping in my ears as I gained control of my breathing. Klei still hadn't returned. I padded into the room and found the silver key in a pale white box.

Then Father screamed.

I followed his screams all the way to the room in a rush.

Klei hollered soon after.

Father was clutching at his face as I stepped in the doorway. Red ichor leaked between his fingers. In the dim light, Klei sprawled on the floor.

"You bitch! I am going to make you regret ever laying a finger on me!" Father stomped over to her and launched a kick at her ribs. Shattered glass covered the floor.

The glass crunched under me like fallen snow as I ran over, grabbed him, and pulled him away from her.

His elbow cut through the air and cracked my eye.

I tumbled to the ground. Black and white dots filled my vision. I blinked rapidly, trying to clear them.

"You? My own son out to kill me? I knew I should have fed you to the dogs!"

I covered my head with my arms as he kicked and stomped at me.

"You damn!" Kick. "Dirty!" Stomp. "No good—"

A roar shook the room. The onslaught stopped.

My ears rang as I shook. My eye swelled to the point where I couldn't open it. Not that I was trying. I cut my palms as I lowered them to the floor.

Klei walked towards me, clutching at her ribs. "Come Young One." She bent over to help me up.

Over her shoulder, dark splatters covered the room. The walls. The floor. The ceiling. I felt the same warm substance seep into my clothes as she lifted me up.

53

"What did you do?" Fear turned my insides cold.

She stayed quiet as she led me out of the room.

* * *

As we rushed outside a sense of numbness overwhelmed me. The dread Father held over the manor was gone, yet an equal frost took his place. What happens to me now?

"Stay close behind me," Klei whispered over her shoulder. The shacks grew closer.

"What do we do?"

"When we pass the guards, you will have to unlock us from our restraints. I cannot."

"No, I mean when this is over." I stopped and waited for her to turn around. "What happens?"

"When this is over, we will be free to go and make our own fate."

Her answer settled in my stomach like a rock.

"I know this isn't what you wanted, Young One. We didn't want this either. We need to see this through." She paused to let me digest. "You ready?"

I nodded. My choice was already made for me.

* * *

Men's voices talked inside the first shack we passed. Light poured out of the doorway and the nearby lanterns. A pale, heavy man stood just outside of the entrance, a long musket gripped tightly in his hand. We avoided him easily as he was almost sleeping where he stood. We snuck down

54

the dirt path where the same stench from before clouded around us.

"In here." Klei pointed at the pristine reflective door ahead of us. Even the rot around the hinges was erased.

A deathly silence made my movements even louder.

Klei never made a sound.

I pulled the key from my pocket and jammed it into the lock. A heavy thud vibrated through me as I turned the key.

With the Moon's light blocked there was only pure blackness in front of me, but I felt their eyes. A hushed whisper circled me as I inched deeper. The rancid smell burned my nose and throat. A few of them attempted to subdue their coughing but failed.

I don't want to curse you along with me.

I stopped and turned back to the entrance to hand Klei the key and wait.

"You should do this." I whispered.

She walked past me and joined the shadow in the room. Within moments their locks fell to the floor. Klei walked out to meet me outside.

"You should leave before you get hurt."

"Hurt?"

"You are Father's son. You have aided us, but that doesn't make you one of us." She pulled me to the side as the Hollow walked out. Dozens of them surrounded us, each of them looking to Klei. This was only one shack. Plenty more waited for her.

"Goodbye, Young One."

Klei backed away and the others followed. With her back to me, she worked the lock behind her mask. The jaguar facade dropped to the ground as she walked to the other

55

buildings, key in hand. She brushed past the doors and came out with more and more people each time.

I sat in the shack and watched them storm the guards. They didn't even get to fire their muskets. The rancid smell soon turned to smoke as fire spread through the manor. A few coughs tore through me as the smoke thickened.

* * *

When the sun came over the horizon, hundreds of masks littered the ground. I avoided the few bodies that collected in the dirt on my way to the burning embers of Brenner manor. I picked up Klei's jaguar before walking down the path lined with oak trees. My finger hovered over the blood on one of its teeth. I thought better of it and left the mark, tucking it under my arm to cough. I didn't bother looking behind me as I walked away from the manor. Only the rotting shacks were left standing.

Before long, the smell of smoke was replaced by the sun-kissed flora and the dry smell of earth. Up ahead in the distance my feeling of hope grew as the blurry outline of horses trotted closer. A light smile cracked my dry lips as I waved my arms around. My throat has been dry since the night before. It's hoof beats became louder as I focused on what was familiar.

"Is that..."

Luis led two other equines behind him, each ridden by a man in dark clothing. I froze. The sun bounced off their faces in a harsh glare. The circle of red around their eyes stole my gaze. Only now in the brightest light of day could I see them clearly.

Unmasked.

All too quickly they came to a halt in front of me. Each of them looked down at me. My limbs bound to my sides, my feet turned to stone, eyes drying as I didn't dare blink. Their gaze rested on the jaguar under my arm. Harsh whispers came out of their mouths, and despite how loud they were, I couldn't understand them. Louder and louder they roared, overwhelming my thoughts and ricocheting in my skull. Finally, my eyes squeezed shut. Harsher, louder, their voices cut into me.

Klei's presence was long gone. I clutched the mask close, praying mercy still resonated within it.

Dedication

I am privileged to say thank you to my family for supporting me in every aspect of my life. Without you, I would not be here today nor would I be the free spirit I pride myself on. Although my story may leave quite a few questions rattling around in your head, I am honored to have the opportunity to share my voice in this anthology. Even though this story is fiction, there are even scarier monsters in our world who will put you down at every opportunity. If you gain the fortitude to be yourself, there will always be others in this world to fight for you as well.

The Wolf Crown

by
Kerith Fontenault

Prince. Did he deserve that title? Since his father died, what had he done for his people? Nothing. He had done nothing for them—the real rulers were his Regents. He could have their power if he wished, but this situation was better for the people. Maybe he wasn't ruling them, but he was still protecting them.

Protecting them from himself.

Leaving the country in others' hands, the prince had sunk back into the darkness. He talked to no one. Ate little, slept less.

It went on for months with no improvement.

His condition grew worse. The doctors thought it was poor health, but the prince knew better. Slowly his state of mind degraded. He became...wolfish. He knew what was happening to him, but he didn't care. Not that he could've done anything about it even if he did. Maybe the change could have been slowed, but not stopped. It would overcome him eventually and he would be all wolf—in mind and in body. On the outside, he looked normal but inside he was changing, and changing fast.

Lost in his thoughts, he stared out the high window. All the colors seemed dark and muted. Had the rolling hills ever had color? The whole countryside was muted grays and browns. At this time of year, the sun should be shining down, glinting off the bright green grass. But it wasn't. It didn't. Was it just him?

58

"Prince Seir, please. You haven't eaten all day. Come and—"

Seir spun around. His neck prickled, and his vision sharpened, zeroing in on the throat. In one fluid movement he drew his dagger and lunged at the servant, then stopped short. His vision returned to normal and he shook himself.

The servant stood, staring at Seir in a startled silence. His mouth hung open and his fingers twitched nervously, unsure how to react.

For the first time Seir registered the weapon he held, then let it clatter to the ground.

His voice was hoarse and cracked when he spoke. "I'm sorry." He hung his head.

The servant glanced at him, fear still clouding his eyes. "M—my prince. Are you alright?"

"Yes."

"Perhaps I should tell the Regents. If anything's wrong they're the ones to talk to."

"No!" His neck prickled once more, this time sending a sharp throb down his spine. He reined himself in. "No. They cannot know. I'm capable of helping myself. Leave me in peace."

"You must eat at some point. The Regents say so."

Seir raised his eyebrows. "I could always eat right now. My Regents are always so thoughtful, sending me snacks throughout the day."

The servant left in a hurry.

Seir sighed. How much longer would it be before the wolf claimed him completely? What would happen in the meantime?

59

He retrieved his dagger from where it lay on the stone floor. Light glinted off the blade and the engraving on it caught Seir's eye. Before the king gave it to him, he'd had the words 'never stop fighting' inscribed on it.

As the heir to the throne, he'd said, *your life will be riddled with troubles. But if you fight and never stop, you will be able to keep your throne and carry on our family line.*

As a child, Seir had soaked up every word that came from his father's mouth.

Now, looking at that inscription, Seir felt a twinge of guilt. He had done exactly what his father had told him not to. He'd stopped fighting. But why should he feel guilty about not fighting if there was no reason for it? Why fight anymore when you know you're going to lose? What's the point?

Seir walked to the great hall. He felt exhausted. Why did he get so tired every time he went crazy? He stopped outside the door. Something was off. His vision sharpened again, and the exhaustion faded, though nothing seemed wrong.

The change must've been quickening. Every time he lost it, the changes grew.

Well, there was no way to find out if something was wrong apart from opening the door and going in.

Seir swung the doors open.

No one was there. No other people around. This was how he liked it. He could be alone with his thoughts.

As he walked into the room his vision stayed sharp. His footsteps boomed. Why were they so loud? The change must've been doing something to his hearing.

The high ceiling arched overhead, held up with intricately carved pillars. Richly embroidered tapestries covered the walls. The stories they depicted were all but forgotten, only the oldest of minstrels remembered their ancient tales. Down the center of the room ran a large stone table. It had been carved from many blocks of stone, but they had been fit together so there was barely a seam.

At the end of the table, a place had been laid out for Seir. In the king's seat. Where his father used to sit. Why would they do that? Seir's place was next to him, by his side, not stealing his place and pretending as if everything was normal.

Nothing was normal. His father had been assassinated, and he'd lied to the people to keep the peace at his Reagents' urging.

A breeze wafted through the single window at the back of the room, layered with things it could've told him, yet he couldn't quite figure out how to read it.

The pins and needles in his neck grew sharper, like they'd poke through his skin at any moment. A faint whistle sliced the air. Seir whipped toward the glint of steel hurtling towards him, snatched the knife from the air and charged his attacker.

He focused on the power running through his limbs. He felt strong, the strongest he had for a long time. Powerful, yet not in control. He slammed his attacker against the wall and pinned it there. Shining daggers, black clothing, dark mask. The traditional dress for an assassin.

"Thought you could do away with me?" His face contorted in a grin. "Well, you thought wrong. Don't you have anything to say for yourself?"

"Nothing interesting," a female voice answered.

Seir almost let go, but the wolf held him steady. "What a joke. Who would send a *girl* to kill someone?" His voice sounded angry even to his own ears.

He reached up to pull her mask off, but she yanked one of her arms out from under him and grabbed his wrist with a gloved hand. Her grip was surprisingly strong.

"To answer your question, someone smarter than you."

She let go of him and he pulled off the mask. Her raw umber eyes unnerved him.

She smirked, then moved in a blur. Seir fell into the wall, then spun to face her.

She stood a few yards behind him, a smug look on her face. "Come on, Prince. You're so easy to distract." She flipped his dagger in the air and caught it.

The animal anger and senses were receding. Of course. The one time they would've actually been helpful was right when they left. The strength that came along with the beast disintegrated. A wave of exhaustion crashed over him, he staggered, everything blurred, then went black.

* * *

Seir awoke on the hard ground. He squeezed his eyes shut, trying to remember what had happened. Something about a girl assassin...Why wasn't he dead right now? Maybe she wanted a ransom.

"Are you trying to convince me you're still asleep? Because I'm not buying it."

Seir looked around. He was in a small dark room, leaned against a rough wall.

"Ready yet?" She lifted a satchel off the ground.

62

"That depends on what you're asking if I'm ready for."

She glared, not at anything in particular. "Come on. Let's go." Her voice had gone from its previous amusement, to a serious tone in the course of two sentences. Didn't seem like the best of signs.

He could try to escape, but he was unarmed. She on the other hand, was armed to the teeth. As if to prove his point she took a knife out of her belt. An attempt at escape would most likely end in his death. Not really what he was going for.

Seir stood. "Where are we going?" Did he really expect her to answer that? Why was he talking to the person who had just kidnapped him anyway?

She slung her bag over her shoulder. "It's not far. That way."

Seir walked in the direction she pointed, down a dirt road with a few houses on either side. When he looked over his shoulder, he could see the castle. As the girl walked behind him, she continued speaking.

"Someone really should've shown you this a long time ago. Your people need you right now."

"They don't, and I can't be there for them." And he was still talking. Great.

"Okay, I get that your dad was murdered, but you still have responsibilities."

Seir spun on her. How did she know? No. She couldn't know. She was fishing. "He wasn't murdered. It was a sickness."

"Do you really expect me to believe that when I helped kill him?"

63

Seir didn't have any words, only rage. His attempts to still the wolf inside him were utterly futile. It ripped through his mind, tore through the walls of its cage, and clawed itself to the surface of his consciousness.

The girl stayed calm. "Really Prince? Last time you went crazy like this you were out for at least a few hours. You haven't even seen what I'm going to show you."

"I don't care," he said, but nevertheless the wolf slowed its ascent, and the edge of his mind cleared, allowing for actual thoughts. He should kill her, then he could hunt down the others who had been involved in the murder and so avenge his father. But would that bring him back? What kind of question was that? Of course it wouldn't. It would only result in the loss of more lives.

"Just keep going," she said.

Seir continued on, as thoughts of his father welled up inside him. He had taught him to shoot, gently pushing his elbow down every time it rose too high, never getting impatient. Eventually under his guidance Seir surpassed even his skill. Then there were the countless times they'd riffled through the ancient volumes of lore, trying to be the first to find a story neither of them had heard, his father nearly always being the winner. There were so many things Seir missed about him...

The smell hit Seir before he saw anything. The smell of ashes, rot, and death was overwhelming. Seir stopped.

"No. Keep going," the girl said. "You should've known about this a long time ago."

What was it she kept talking about?

They reached a tall wall with a single door in it. The girl motioned for Seir to step aside, and he obeyed, eyeing her knife. She pulled the door open.

"Go on. It's high time that you be here."

Seir walked through the door. If the smell had been bad outside, it was even worse here. He followed her into a building off one side of the road.

Even if he had been warned ahead of time, nothing could've prepared him for what he saw.

The interior was larger than he expected, yet it felt cramped and hot. Cots lined the walls. Sobs filled the air and the scent of death and blood was so thick that it was hard to breathe. The room was lit only by the few windows and candles that were set along the edge. The light did nothing to lessen the horror. Lean figures lay, curled in pain on the cots, praying their death would come soon.

A few people went from bed to bed, trying to help in any way possible. Not far from where Seir stood in the doorway, sat a cot with a small child on it. A woman leaned over the bed crying. The child's body was racked with a fit of coughing, convulsing in unseen pain.

The coughing slowed and went silent, the thrashing stilled, and the child's body lay limply on the cot. One of the volunteers scooped up the lifeless body and carried it from the room, and the woman ran after the volunteer, wailing for her child.

The girl's hard voice startled him out of his stupor. "Bad. Isn't it?"

"What is this?"

"I'll talk to you outside."

After getting a few houses away from the building the girl stopped and turned to Seir. "This is what your father did. This is what you are doing. Both of you are the same. You are letting the people die."

Seir bared his teeth. "That is a lie!"

"No. It's not. My mother died because of you. I had to watch as she died a slow painful death, all the while knowing that the only thing your father was doing about this plague was spending more money on himself and ignoring the people."

Seir could barely contain his rage. His muscles trembled. The wolf would surface any minute now. "I don't know what you're talking about. My father cared about the people. Why can't you go away and leave me alone?"

"Because the people are dying! If we hadn't gotten rid of him all of them would've died. He didn't listen. He didn't care. He ignored our pleas for help and spent money on huge parties and feasts. His taxes were high and his love for money outweighed his love for his people."

"He would never do that." Seir's neck stung and the world sharpened into crisp lines and details. He didn't want to lose control of his actions, so he fought it as the girl continued talking.

"And you're biased. You didn't meddle in the affairs of the people. He kept you out of them. He wanted an admirer, someone who would look up to him and praise him for being such a good ruler. Now that he's gone the people are still suffering. Your Regents picked up ruling right where your father left off. You are letting the people die. Mothers, fathers, little children. All dead."

66

Seir didn't know what to say to that. The people were dying, that was obvious. Whether or not his father was guilty, they needed help. His mind was clouded from keeping the wolfish rage from surfacing. "I need to think."

"You see what's happening. We had to get rid of the king. He would've let the whole kingdom die of poverty and sickness. What's there to think about? Even if your father didn't help them then, you can help the people now. They need you to rule them and help them through these times."

"I'm not meant to rule the people."

Fierceness kindled in her raw umber eyes. "Do. Better."

She held the hilt of his knife out to him, and he took it, slightly surprised she had kept it, and more surprised she was giving it back to him. "I'm Erin, but I'll be your end if you don't."

Then she walked away, back into the village.

* * *

Seir didn't have much trouble finding his way back to the palace. The hill it perched on loomed far over the countryside, and the castle's huge mass covered the whole crown of it.

Had Erin been telling him the truth? The grief in her eyes had been real, as real as his own. Was what was happening to the people really his father's fault?

When he reached the palace, he went straight to the war room. When it was not being used for meetings of war it was used as a conference room where the king would discuss matters of state. Seir had not been in the room often. When

67

his father was king, he had not been allowed to attend the meetings.

Was it true, what Erin had said about his father shielding him from the truth of what was happening?

Seir stopped outside the room. His Regents were discussing something. Seir recognized the head Regent's voice when he began to speak. His voice sounded strangely giddy.

"We raise the taxes another notch, then, when the people are unable to pay them, we will *allow* them to pay us with their land."

The blanket of white-hot wolfish rage didn't even give Seir a chance to think before he smashed through the doors into the meeting.

All the Regents sitting at the long table, except the head Regent with his back to the door, looked at him, mouths hanging open in shock. Somehow the head Regent didn't notice Seir break into the room and continued talking.

"We can remove the land from their possession and add it to our own personal—" At that moment he looked back and saw Seir, and his mouth hung open to match the rest.

Seir stood in the doorway, chest heaving.

The head Regent stood, glancing nervously around the room. "Your majesty—"

"No." That was his father's title. His spine throbbed. Pain raked his chest. "You knew about the people, didn't you? The plague? And you didn't tell me. You were letting them die, and knowingly making it worse."

"My prince. We were—"

"I don't care what you were going to do."

68

His vision zeroed in on the head Regent, on his sweaty brow and the pulse in his pink neck. Seir ran at him and came to a hard stop inches from his face. He brandished his dagger, voice filled with rage. "You didn't care if all the people died. As long as their money got to you, you didn't care about them."

"Actually—"

Seir was shouting now, his breaths coming quickly. His teeth throbbed and felt strange in his mouth, pushing into his gums and against each other. "No. Stop. you don't have any explanation that can make me believe you. I heard the way you were talking."

"Just let me—"

"No. Get out."

"Get out?"

Seir turned and shouted at the Regents swinging his knife in a wide circle, but their gazes were on his face. His eyes and teeth.

"All of you out! I never want to see any of you again!"

They stood, almost as one, and rushed for the door. The head Regent followed suit, trying to walk away, but Seir moved in front of him to block his path.

Seir's shoulders slumped and his chest heaved. Splitting jabs of pain coursed through his head. Through the mass of chaotic pain and senses he struggled to form a few words. "Is it true? Did father let the people die?"

"I...Well..." The head Regent looked around desperately for an escape route.

Seir shook his head to clear his thoughts. Then focused. "Answer truthfully."

The head Regent swallowed. "Yes. He did."

69

Seir nodded and stepped aside. "Go. Leave."

The head Regent fled after the others.

Seir's vision began to return to normal and his limbs felt limp and exhausted. But he couldn't rest. How could he ever rest again? He walked to the throne room, thoughts of his father pressing for attention as he crossed the great floor.

Seir knelt in front of the throne, head bent in sorrow.

Why did he have to be so lonely? He had no one to guide him, no trusted friends to give him council. If only his father was still alive. He would've been able to tell Seir exactly what to do. He would've laid his hand on Seir's shoulder and helped him through the hard times.

But how much of it would have been lies?

If he were still alive the people would've continued to be neglected. They would've kept dying of sickness. Hunger. Who knew what else. Maybe it was better this way. It didn't feel better, but maybe it was. Now that Seir saw what was happening he could do something about it. Now that he was ruler, he could make the changes his father had refused to.

There was still the problem of becoming a wolf. Sooner or later no matter what he did, it would pull him away from his people and he would have to live alone, forever a wolf, in the dark forest. Realizing his father had done wrong didn't lessen his grief. It wouldn't stop the change. He had been the best father if not the best king. The full picture of him only made the grief howl louder. He had not only lost the best side of him, but also the possibility of ever confronting him about the worst.

* * *

In the coming weeks, Seir made it his top priority to search out new Regents. These were people he deemed to be responsible and trustworthy. People who would take over when he was gone.

With his kingdom out of danger, he took to wandering the streets of the various towns under his rule. Or maybe he was searching. Searching for Erin.

It gave him a purpose. A reason to fight. Maybe he was fighting the inevitable, maybe he would still turn into a wolf, but he could at least make the most of his limited time.

Why her? She aided in the death of his father.

Just as his father aided in her mother's death, and the deaths of countless others.

The brisk wind nipped at Seir's face and sent colorful leaves spinning through the air and scuttling across the ground. He followed the packed dirt path as he kicked stones before him.

His destination came into view. The building extended two stories at the edge of the path, newly constructed as a place for the people to gather for food and healing. Many had been built for this purpose all around the kingdom. The royal treasury had been quite full. It was incredible how the people flourished under the new rule. They were still burdened with sickness and poverty, but they had slowly been making their way back to what they used to be, to what his father had convinced him they were all along.

Seir opened the door, keeping one hand tucked under his cloak. People sat at wooden tables along the edges of the room. A warm fire twinkled in the corner, inviting him to come in out of the chill weather.

"Is there anything I can help you with?" a woman asked when he entered.

"No. Just looking for someone." He sat down at a table in one corner of the room. How much time did he have left? The change was already severe.

"Looking for someone, Prince?"

Seir turned to see Erin where she stood a few feet behind him. She flipped his dagger in the air and caught it.

Success at last. "Could I have my knife back?"

"Sure Prince, why not?" She walked around the edge of the table, stood across from him, and passed him his knife. "You've been looking for me."

There was no surprise in her voice. It was more of a statement than a question.

"Yes. I wanted to apologize. I was harsh towards you."

"It's fine, under the circumstances I probably would've reacted the same way."

Seir sighed. "Of course, my father's death still weighs heavily on me, but I think that maybe it would help to have a friend. You helped me realize that...my father wasn't the best king. If he hadn't been killed, the people would've revolted by now to put a stop to him. So many other people would've died, and still my father might not have lived...It was better this way. For the kingdom."

"When will you be going back to your throne to rule the people? Your changes are all great, but still, it would be better for them if they had a king. Someone steady."

"You don't understand, I *can't* rule them." He drew his hand out from under his cloak. "I've been changing, turning into a wolf."

72

He held his hand up into the light, and Erin stepped back almost knocking over the chair behind her.

The fingers were shriveled and small looking. Coarse dark fur sprouted from the hand and his nails were sharp, pointed claws.

"What's causing the change?"

When Seir looked at Erin he was surprised to see genuine concern on her face.

"It's sadness, I think. The grief over my father's death. No matter how many times I admit it to myself that my father was wrong, the loss never goes away."

"I know how you feel. I lost my mother to the plague. All I felt was rage and hatred toward your father for letting it happen. For letting the people die. When I saw you, Prince, I wondered if you were changing. If that was why you were acting the way you were."

Seir shifted in his chair. Where was she going with this?

"Your father's death was hard." Her raw umber eyes flicked toward his. "I feel you more than you realize."

* * *

Tree branches rustled, their new buds swaying in the air. Fall passed, winter passed, now it was spring.

With only the stars for light, the dark of the new moon filled every crevice of the wood, blanketing it in a still darkness.

The gentle breeze that caressed the countryside ruffled the grass, its cool rustling rising to blend with the mournful song of the crickets.

If one had looked out into the night they might've been able to make out the sleek forms of two wolves trotting side by side into the darkness, and if one had listened they might've heard their calls far into the night. To human ears those calls may have sounded sad and melancholy, but to the ears of wolves, they sounded of ones who had a friendship that would last forever.

In the Coming Tides

by
Brianna Timpson

Crash... crash... crash...

With summer vacation coming to an end, all Anahita could focus on were the crashing waves, their rhythm as familiar as her heartbeat.

Crash... crash... crash...

"C'mon!" Sadie said. "I know you love the waves, so I don't understand why you won't go in the water. Come on, Ana. Do it for me."

Anahita smiled and shook her head, her long, brown hair flying in the wind. "You know the answer is no and it always will be. Go ahead. I'll stay here."

"But it's the last day of summer vacation! You'll be leaving soon, so just put your feet in. It'll be fine."

Anahita stared at the vast ocean and longed to swim, but she wouldn't. She couldn't. She glanced down the beach. It wasn't busy, even though summer was coming to an end. A wave splashed against the shore and another followed. Her stomach dropped with the ebb of the tide. She had to leave.

"You know what? It's really hot out. We should probably head back to your house."

"Which is why we should be going *in* the water." Sadie sighed as she packed up her bag. "Promise me you'll go in the water next time, not just stare at it."

"I make zero promises." Anahita smirked over an edge pain, a skill she'd mastered over a summer of necessary excuses she regretted. Sadie was intuitive, persistent, and stubborn. All the things she liked her for made it so hard to keep her safe.

They walked up the dunes into the parking lot, their feet burning from the sand.

"Ana? Give me a straight answer this time. Why don't you like going in the water?" she asked.

Anahita kicked a smooth beach stone in a glittering spray of pale sand. "If I had a nickel for every time you've asked me that question, I'd be a millionaire."

"Straight answer, remember?"

Anahita hesitated at the dogged persistence in Sadie's eyes. Maybe her parents were right, and she should have been more careful about getting to know this girl. About letting this girl know her. "It's the seaweed. It just feels so weird and your feet get caught in it."

"But that still doesn't explain why you won't go in the pool!"

"Is your mom picking us up or are we walking?" It pained Anahita to have to do this with her best friend.

"Walking. She's helping a neighbor." She paused to look in her bag. "Want to make a quick stop first?"

"Where to?"

"There's a booth up the street selling lemonade. I'm low on water."

They walked up the street while the sound of the waves grew fainter behind them. They stopped at a crosswalk and waited for the light to turn green. The sun was so hot at midday; there were more cars than pedestrians, but a man in black with glossy shades caught her eye. Anahita's pulse skipped with dread and she snapped her attention back to the light. A drop of sweat inched down her temple as her anxiety climbed.

The light turned green.

Anahita rushed across the street and Sadie followed with a frown.

"What was *that* all about? What's the rush?"

"It's nothing. Where's the booth?"

"Darn it. It should be right here. It must've gotten too hot."

The man approached the light and Anahita gasped. A woman with many piercings and another man with longer hair than the first followed. They were all dressed in black. Maybe she should've stayed home. Maybe it was someone else who was supposed to do this.

Sadie looked back. "What are you looking at?"

"Umm... I just noticed what time it was. I can't believe it's nearly two! Let's keep moving." Of course, Sadie wasn't worried. They could only be seen by someone if they wanted to.

They continued to walk toward Sadie's house, a bit faster than normal. The trio stopped trailing them about half-way there. Anahita peered into every alley and store window on their way. Where did they go? Why stop now? As they were about to go inside, the trio reappeared a few houses back.

"Umm... you know what? There's a really good ice cream parlor just a few blocks down. Want to stop?" Anahita asked without taking her gaze off the trio. Why did she come here with Sadie? She should have gone off on her own, and they would have let Sadie be. They weren't after her.

"What do you mean? We just got here."

"Do you trust me?" Anahita asked, looking Sadie in the eyes. Her chin trembled slightly.

"What? Of course, I do."

"Then if I tell you we need to leave, will you leave?"

"Not without reason, no. Tell me. What's going on?"

77

"I didn't want to do this. I really didn't. I'm sorry." Anahita clutched Sadie's tanned wrist. She mumbled under her breath in her native tongue, then raised her voice. *"C'mon, Sadie. Let's go get some ice cream."*

Sadie's eyes went wide with shock, but she nodded and followed Anahita. Regret welled in Anahita's stomach, but she had no other option.

Anahita checked behind her as they headed down the driveway. The trio pursued.

She should have stuck to the plan, stayed isolated and unattached, the perfect bait with no complications in the way of her goal. Now she had a really big complication.

The block before the parlor, Anahita lost sight of their pursuers. Her pulse slowed. She pulled Sadie as they ducked down an alley.

Anahita spoke in her native tongue again, then nibbled on her lip. Sadie jerked back as the compulsion dropped and almost screamed. She clapped her hand over Sadie's mouth, grabbed her wrist, and sat her down on the ground. Sadie struggled and tried to scream for help.

"Hush! Do you want to be killed? If I release you, you can't run or scream," Anahita whispered, her voice filled with dread.

Sadie nodded and Anahita released her.

"What is wrong with you!? What's going on!?"

Anahita clapped her hand over Sadie's mouth again. "Quiet! It's not safe here." She let go.

"Then why are we here?"

"Hiding."

"Why?"

"I want to tell you. I *will* tell you. Just not now, not here." She paused. "Stay here." Anahita walked to the entrance of the alley. She glanced up and down the street.

The trio had their backs turned to inspect the dark windows of a storefront. They had to move fast. Anahita motioned to Sadie. "C'mon, before they see us."

"Before *who* sees us?"

"Answers later. Escaping now."

They rushed out of the alleyway then down the road. When they reached a small patch of forest, Anahita checked for pursuers. There was no one in sight...none of *them* at least. They headed into the middle of the grove and sat down. Sadie's cheeks were sunburned, and her black hair stuck to her face. Anahita couldn't look into her eyes.

"Tell me what's going on," Sadie demanded, panting.

"It would be easier to show you, but I doubt you're ready. I'd become a science project if I told you."

"Ready? Ready! You're my best friend. I'm *always* ready for anything you have to tell me." She shook her head. "Like in a psych ward. Yeah, maybe."

"Ha. Not a psych ward. I'm not insane." Anahita rolled her eyes and looked up at the treetop, then sighed. "I've lied to you. I love swimming. I just… can't. Not in public at least."

"Are you *that* bad at swimming?"

"No." Anahita laughed and sat down on the soft grass. "I was born swimming. Like you, swimming is my life. The ocean… it's just so serene."

Sadie waited, but Anahita didn't continue. What was she doing? She couldn't tell Sadie, she'd only actually known her for a couple months, but as dangerous as revealing her secret was for herself, it was more dangerous for Sadie to not know now that she was in danger.

"So… what's the secret? And before you answer that, what in the world did you just do to me? It was like I couldn't control my body."

"It's a form of hypnosis. You did what I wanted you to. You were silent and you nodded. That's all that mattered."

Sadie was silent for a long time. She unscrewed her water bottle and took a sip. "And the first part?"

"Those people... they hunt people like me. They're not human. They're like me, but also not like me."

She laughed. "Okay, joke's over." Sadie grabbed Anahita's wrist. "Stop playing. If you don't want to be my friend, that's fine. Just tell me. Tell me the truth."

"Sadie. I'm not lying. It's the truth. I'm not human."

Sadie dumped the rest of her water bottle on Anahita's head.

Anahita finally met Sadie's gaze and sighed. "I didn't want it to happen this way." Her legs grew warm, then hot and started to merge while webbing sprouted between her toes. A rush of teal scales flowed over her legs and her shorts melted into the fabric and her shirt changed into a shimmering bikini top as the glamor unraveled. She curled her sparkling, teal tail. A fishtail. A mermaid tail.

Sadie closed her eyes and pinched herself, then looked again. Nothing changed. She inched away from Anahita.

"How?" Sadie shook her head.

Anahita fiddled with the grass then whispered, "I'm a rose moon mermaid." She drew a steadying breath. "I was born under a full moon, giving me the ability to go on land."

Sadie half-laughed, half-choked with tears. "Mermaids aren't real. There's no such thing as magic."

"Sadie, stop it. Stop it!"

Sadie kneeled and shook her head. "No such thing... mermaids don't exist."

"Sadie..." Anahita gently took Sadie's hand and placed it on her tail. "It's real. I'm real."

Sadie looked up at Anahita with wide, but soft eyes and nodded. "I'm sorry."

Anahita smiled. "No need. *I'm* sorry." She paused. "Remember when we first met?

Sadie nodded. "I was being pushed around by a bully from school. You stood up to him."

"That's not how we first met."

"We literally met on the last day of school. You came here on vacation."

"No. We met earlier. We met six years ago. We were eight. You were swimming too far out in the ocean, but your mom got distracted. She didn't see you."

Sadie's brow creased. "How do you know that?"

"You almost drowned, but someone saved you. You didn't see them, but they helped you back to shore."

"It was the tide. It couldn't have been you...could it?"

"Yeah... I was lost, too. I floated away from class and saw you. I guess there was a reason for that."

"How did you recognize me?"

"You might not have seen me, but I saw you. Now is not the time for sentimentality, though."

"Right. So, who were they? Who are we running from?"

Anahita fidgeted with her fingers. "Sirens," she whispered.

"Sirens?" Sadie paused. "Mermaid, Siren. Po-tay-to, pa-tah-to."

"Not po-tay-to, pa-tah-to. More like reaper pepper, tomato."

"I'm not following. Both have tails, both live in the sea. I don't see any difference."

"Sirens come from one, special mermaid. She was a winged mermaid that could change her appearance. One of her ancestors had an enchanted voice that she inherited. The

81

Siren had committed a crime, though it's unclear what it was. Some say that she stole the trident of Poseidon. Others say that she killed a merfolk ruler. Whatever she did, it must have been really serious. Poseidon punished her and all of her descendants. He ripped her wings and tail off, along with her enchanted voice." Anahita looked back up at the treetops. "Legend has it, the only way for them to regain all of their powers is to kill a mermaid, but not just any mermaid. Poseidon also cursed a line of merpeople to make it more difficult, I guess. Only one merperson a generation would receive the curse, though. That merperson would be born under a full moon at the beginning of May. They would either remove the curse and their powers for good, *or* restore them. No other mermaid would work."

Sadie shuffled slightly. "And you're that mermaid… Warning, I have a lot of questions, and I mean a lot. For starters, what was her name?"

"No one knows for sure. Some say it was Sirena. The names have been mixed up through the centuries."

"Are there only female Sirens?"

"Some have bred with humans, so there are males and females." Anahita looked down at her tail as it dried. Her tail separated into legs and her regular clothes reappeared. Soon, the scales faded and her legs were back to normal. "We should get going before they find us."

"How are they tracking us?"

"It's like a Siren sixth sense. They know when mermaids are near."

"So… where are we going?"

"I'm not sure yet. I just know we are avoiding fantasy hangouts."

"Fantasy hangouts? Like mythological creatures?"

"Not myths, really. Hangouts for people like werewolves, vampires... and Sirens."

"Wait, wait, wait." She held up her hand. "Werewolves and vampires exist? Since when?" Sadie said, almost throwing her backpack.

"Since forever? I don't know!" She thought for a moment. "My grandmother was once friends with a human. He lives in a tent along the shore of Caspian Beach and had all kinds of potions and spells. I was supposed to get a piece of a Siren, blood or hair or even spit and take it to him, but that seems too dangerous now, but maybe he can help us some other way, or at least help protect you."

"And wizards, too? What else?"

"Where do you think legends came from? People actually saw these things."

"You're telling me, Nessie and Bigfoot and... and... zombies are real?"

"I'd rather not answer that." Anahita smirked, though her stomach lurched a bit. She had said too much. "C'mon."

The girls went back into town. Caspian Beach was on the opposite side of town, so the girls hopped on a bus.

"Where to?" asked the bus driver.

"Two tickets to Caspian Beach, please."

"Ten dollars."

Sadie handed him the money. The bus driver's arm was filled with tattoos and he smelled strongly of alcohol. Sadie and Anahita gave each other nervous glances. They started down the road, but the bus took a wrong turn. A turn back in the direction they had come from.

"Siren," Anahita whispered. She should've known something was wrong when the others stopped following. "We have to get off of here."

"It's just a wrong turn."

Anahita glanced up and down the aisle. There were only two other people on the bus. They were both girls, similar enough to be twins with platinum blonde hair. They wore all black.

"Sirens."

Sadie looked, too. The bus ground to a stop. Anahita's heart pounded. The door opened. They both seemed to know what the other was thinking and they bolted for the door. The twins ran forward, too. The bus driver held out his arm, but Anahita ducked and yanked his hair and tore a few strands free from his scalp. He pulled his arm back with a yell, and they darted past. Sadie and Anahita apologized as they pushed through the group of people that were boarding. A few bus stops away, the girls found another bus. No one wore black this time.

* * *

Once they arrived, they headed towards the quiet side of the beach, which was empty, except for one tent. The wizard's tent.

"There it is!" Anahita exclaimed.

"What? Where?"

"It's literally right there! Like five feet in front of you."

"It's sand. All sand." Shaking her head, Sadie grabbed a flat, gray rock and was about to skip it when a voice stopped her.

"I wouldn't do that if I were you. You'll attract unwanted attention."

Sadie turned and looked about, but saw no one. A smiling man with a long, gray beard and hair to match it, approached them. He wore a red top paired with old, ripped jeans. Around his neck hung a gold chain necklace with an

84

odd, gold charm attached. The charm had a pattern like a dream catcher, but more intricate. Small stars studded the intersections of the lines. In the center, the pattern almost looked like a wave.

"Mermaids. Sirens." He looked thoughtfully at the waves. "You don't want anyone else on your case, do you?" He glanced at Anahita. "I know your grandmother. A beautiful rose moon mermaid, like you. We used to be friends, Aquata and I. I fell for her a hundred times over. Oh, but you're not here to hear about an old man's life. How can I help you in the coming tides?"

"Huh? Where are you?" Sadie questioned.

"He's standing in front of you Sadie."

"Oh, yes, dear child. You wish to see me, Sadie?" Sadie yelped as the wizard appeared in front of her. He chuckled. "Good ol' Siren charm; Hides you unless you want to be seen. You can call me Silas." He looked back at Anahita. "You should try to conceal your identity better, you know. A knowledgeable person could tell you were a mermaid from a mile away."

Anahita smiled slightly. "And any knowledgeable person could tell you were a wizard." She laughed. "Silas, my grandmother told me you know about the Siren Curse? That you might be able to help if I brought you something from one of them?"

"Dear girl, I know more than I should. But that is not a matter to be discussed here, Anahita."

"How do you know my name?"

"Your grandmother spoke of you. I wish I could see her more. That's why my tent is here, to see her, but she's happier in the ocean. You look just like her when she was your age. Come, come now. We mustn't waste any time if you wish to remove the Siren Curse."

Silas ushered them through the entrance of his tent and everything changed. The space inside was massive like a mansion. The first room looked like the living room of a family home, but the second looked more like a laboratory. The lab was full of colorful bottles and books. Neither room contained any chairs as far as they could see, only pillows. Sadie picked up one of the bottles, but set it back down after reading the label. The girls sat down on the pillows. The old man sorted through a pile of books and sat down on a pillow, holding a book titled *Creatures, Curses, and Legends: Sea Edition*. He flipped through the pages until he found what looked like a recipe.

"The potion itself is not very difficult," he said. "I have all the ingredients here, assuming you did manage to get what your grandmother asked?"

Anahita reached into her pocket and produced a few dark strands of the bus driver's hair.

"Excellent." Silas grabbed a bottle of water and poured some on Anahita's leg.

"What was that for?! Aren't we trying to not spill my identity?" Anahita shouted as she pulled a towel out of Sadie's bag and transformed.

"Like I said, I have all the ingredients." Silas grabbed a pair of tweezers and plucked one of Anahita's scales.

"Ouch!" Anahita exclaimed as she pulled her tail away from Silas. She wasn't sure if he was nuts or just a jokester with an odd sense of humor.

"You alright?" Sadie asked. Anahita nodded.

"The piece, Anahita." She handed him the hair of the bus driver. Silas dropped the ingredients into a vile and shook it. "There. You have to get a full-blood Siren to drink this. It will remove the curse from all Sirens, along with all of their abilities."

"Permanently?" asked Anahita.

Silas nodded.

"I get that the Sirens are evil, but why permanently? Grant them their powers and they're no longer evil, right? They'd have no reason to come after you," Sadie said.

Anahita avoided Sadie's gaze. "They've taught themselves some limited spells, like the invisibility, but they use merfolk to do it. They kidnapped me and many other merkids. They almost killed me to remove my magic to fuel theirs. If they get their true powers back, it will be easy for them to hunt us down and strip our magic to fuel even greater power. If they're trapped on land, most of my people will be safe."

"You're kidding! Oh, Ana, I'm so sorry."

"I'm one of the cursed ones. I think it's my destiny. Ever since I came on land, I've been looking for a way to defeat them."

"Anahita, dear girl, there is a price. Magic is never free, and breaking a curse this old…it's big magic. To break the curse and strip their powers, you'll lose your own. You won't be able to come on land again. You must sacrifice that ability."

"I…" Anahita's voice broke, "I can't go on land?"

"Or you must sacrifice your tail. The gift of the moon will transfer to the potion to activate it. You have until sundown to be in the water or on land, permanently."

Anahita nodded. "Okay, I'll do it." Her heart broke. The price was worth the result.

"Ana, no!"

"I've got no choice."

"You know the old warehouse? Anahita should know the one. Go there and be careful." He gave them the potion then stood up and walked away.

"Okay, then," said Sadie. "Odd fellow, isn't he?"

"Pretty much goes for all old wizards." She avoided eye-contact. "Wise and odd."

The girls trekked to the warehouse. Anahita insisted they walk together, one final time. When they arrived, the warehouse looked abandoned. Plants climbed the sides and the few windows were boarded up. No human had set foot there for almost thirty years, only Sirens, and the place hummed with the build-up of all their small charms and stolen magic.

The girls stood watching the building. A door swung open and they ducked behind a bush. A girl about the same age as Sadie and Anahita stepped out. The girl wore her red hair in a ponytail and had a big ring on her finger. She looked around as if she knew someone was there, then shrugged and went back inside.

"How do we know which ones are full-bloods?" asked Sadie.

"One of my teachers used to say that girl Sirens are pure and the boys are half. Don't know how true it is though." Anahita looked at the door. "It's the main entrance. Maybe there's a back door. Wait here." She stood up and walked around the building.

She returned a couple minutes later after dealing with the guard. Sadie spotted the bruise blossoming across her knuckles and started to speak, but Anahita cut her off.

"I'm fine. There's another door in the back. I was able to get it opened, but a Siren came out, hence the bruise. We should be able to get in that way."

Sadie picked up a few stones and loaded them into her pockets. Anahita pulled off a couple of prickly branches from one of the bushes, then they headed inside. The warehouse was loaded with weapons on one wall. Some of

88

them looked like guns or bows and arrows or spears. Other weapons looked like they were from another world. They had odd markings and multiple crystals on the ends. The other wall was bare except for a bit of graffiti and the name of the old warehouse, *Sam's Market.*

The girls peeked into what looked like an old storage room. Flies zoomed around the room and it smelled of mold and rot.

BANG!

A loud noise echoed around the warehouse.

BANG! BANG!

Someone knew they were there and they wanted to scare them away. It almost sounded like a bat hitting a metal wall.

BANG!

The noise sounded farther away. Sadie and Anahita laid flat against one of the walls.

BANG!

Footsteps rounded the corner. The girl with the ring was there, but they couldn't tell if she had seen them.

BANG! BANG!

The girl wasn't the one making the noise, but she held a bow and arrow. Anahita motioned for Sadie to follow her as she inched towards a second door.

BANG!

Anahita jumped from the volume.

BANG!

Then everything went black.

* * *

Anahita's head pounded and there was a sharp pain in the side of her neck. She didn't know what happened. She shook her head and went to scratch her wrist, but she couldn't move her arm. She couldn't move at all.

"Shide?" Anahita's voice was muffled. She tried again. "Syda?" Her mouth was taped shut. A light flickered on and revealed a bunch of people, but some looked like doubles.

"Awake, are we?" asked one of the men. Anahita spotted a tattoo on his arm, but she couldn't tell what it was. "I should kill you now."

"You can't without Carlisle," reminded a red-headed girl. Anahita recognized the ring on her finger.

Her vision started to improve. There were five people. Anahita saw the weapons on the wall behind her. They were back in the main room.

"Oh, well. She'll have to get another mermaid. This one's mine! I'm the eldest."

"No, no, and no. *I* made you a group. *You* let a merkid escape. *You* don't deserve your power. This one's ours," corrected a black-haired woman as she entered the room. The other Sirens bowed.

"Carlisle, I didn't mean…"

"Enough! Shell, take him away. Wipe his memory and send him to-"

"Germany?" piped in another woman who wore a black dress.

"Why not. Do it to Kerry, too. I think she'll enjoy it there."

"No, please. Carlisle, no!" pleaded the first male.

"Oh, no. Please!" begged the girl.

"Away!"

Shell looked, and smelled, like the bus driver they had met earlier. He dragged the two people away as they begged.

"What shall I use to kill you?" asked Carlisle, more to herself than Anahita.

Anahita tried to feel for a knot, but it was just out of reach. While doing so, she looked over at Sadie, who was still slumped in her chair.

"What's your name, girl?" Carlisle asked as she removed the tape over Anahita's mouth, but she didn't speak. Her dark hair fell in front of Anahita's face. "Ah. Shy. Shame." She nodded at one of her followers. "Kill the other."

"Anahita. I'm Anahita," she whispered.

"She can talk! Not yet, Ally." Carlisle held up her hand to stop her follower. "Ever heard of the Siren Curse, Anahita?"

"Get away from me. Every merkid is told that story."

"Then you know the only way to break the curse is to kill a rose moon mermaid. The curse breakers though, are rare, only one each generation in a certain line."

"There can be other ways."

Carlisle gripped Anahita's face. "But only one way to get back what is our birthright. Look at these pathetic legs. They aren't mine. *I* have a tail. *I* have wings. *I* have an enchanted voice. All of that is mine, but *I* can't have them!"

"Ahmta?" asked Sadie.

"Don't say anything! Trust me." Anahita squirmed in Carlisle's grip, then kicked her.

"Oh, ho! Feisty, quiet, and shy. Quite a combo you got there. How's it feeling?" She slid her hand across the sore part of Anahita's neck. "Sleeping darts."

Anahita winced in pain. "Maybe you should try them sometime. I'll make a deal with you. Release Sadie unharmed and you can have me. I won't fight. You don't need her."

"Tempting, but I'll make a counter-offer. I still take you. The other girl will be released, but her memory of you and this," she motioned her hands around the room, "will be removed. Deal?"

"Deal. Now, let her go."

Ally looked at Carlisle then untied Sadie and ripped off the tape. Ally started to pull her out of the room. "Say goodbye to your friend."

"Don't do this! Don't do this, Anahita!"

"Goodbye, Sadie. I don't want anyone else to be harmed." A tear crawled down Anahita's face, but she wouldn't look at Sadie.

Carlisle smiled. "Let's start then." She spun the chair around towards the weapons wall. "Take your pick."

"Poison."

Sadie cried. "Ana, no!" She elbowed Ally in the ribs and Ally doubled over. She rushed over to Anahita and untied her ropes. Carlisle crossed her arms, but didn't protest and Anahita didn't move. She could still save Sadie. What was Sadie doing?

"Three to two. Almost even."

"Three? No, no, dear girl. I think you miscounted." More Sirens poured into the room. Carlisle pushed Anahita's head back and grabbed a vial of poison. "You could've gone free, Sadie. Any final words, girls?"

Anahita laced her voice with magic. "Three. *Watch your back.*" Carlisle looked behind her and Anahita slammed her head into Carlisle.

"Brat!"

The Sirens started to close in.

"We had a deal. Let Sadie go."

"This deal is broken." She uncapped the poison. "A shame, because dead humans are so much more trouble than dead mermaids. But we'll deal with it."

Sadie backed up against the weapons wall and grabbed a bow and arrow. She waved the bow and arrow around, ready to fire. "Stay back!"

The Sirens didn't listen. They came closer. Anahita closed her mouth, refusing to open.

"It'll hurt less if you cooperate," Carlisle snarled.

Sadie released the arrow and it shot over Carlisle's shoulder.

"I won't miss next time."

Carlisle released Anahita and approached Sadie. "Maybe you'd like to join her."

Sadie loaded another arrow. "I won't miss this time."

Carlisle smiled. "You wouldn't do that."

"I would." She released the arrow and it hit Carlisle's chest.

Carlisle screamed in agony and collapsed. Sadie rushed over to Anahita, bow loaded, and she finally stood up.

"Get them!" ordered Carlisle, before she coughed and sprayed the concrete floor with blood.

The Sirens drew closer and closer. The girls backed up towards Carlisle.

"Slip her the potion."

"Anahita, there has to be another wa—"

"Just do it!"

Sadie hesitated, but closed in on Carlisle. The Siren tried to fight, tried to push Sadie back, but Sadie grabbed the shaft of the arrow and wrestled her down. She forced the potion down her throat when Carlisle opened her mouth to scream. Carlisle coughed and sputtered, then went slack.

The Sirens collapsed and screamed in horror as their appearances changed. Ally's hair turned dark brown and her ring slid off her finger, and Carlisle turned old and gray.

Anahita and Sadie pushed the Sirens out of their way as they ran to the ocean. The sun was almost down.

"Here." Anahita handed Sadie a small shell necklace as a tear slipped down her face. "Take it and wear it. Blow into the biggest shell when you want to see me. I'll be looking for a way back to land."

"Thank you. I'll miss you." Sadie fought back tears.

Anahita smiled and walked into the surf as the sun went down.

Sadie couldn't hide her tears anymore. She waded into the ocean and waved.

"Just like her grandmother," Silas said to himself as he approached.

Sadie jumped. "Silas...I want to help her. There has to be a way, can you teach me?"

Silas smiled. "You have the spark deep inside of you, but that spark needs kindling to become a flame. I can help you collect it."

Sadie looked down to the shell necklace in her hand and smiled. A note fell out of the biggest shell.

Best friends are inseparable.

Fading Orange

by
Linden Philo

I'm sweaty and cold. Like every morning. My dreams have been chilling ever since Vincent died. It was never supposed to happen like that.

Vincent's Effect Cube must have malfunctioned, everyone whispers in tones that make me want to rip off my ears.

A loud bark jars me. It's Willow. She wants to go on a walk. Guess I can't really stay in bed all day. The concrete stairs are cold to my bare feet.

I slip into my shoes, grab the leash, and Willow follows me to the door. A shadow blocks the way. I sigh and brace for the onslaught of Dad's next lecture.

"Charlie, I'm so glad you're out of bed. I wanted to have a talk with you."

"Sure, Dad, but I have to take Willow on a walk." I try to sound upbeat.

He ignores the fact I'm walking out the door. "I'm worried about you. You're almost eighteen, and a girl your age should *not* be sitting in her room all day. Your Effect Cube placement is only two days away. This should be a time of celebration!"

"Dad, I don't want to keep talking about this. I've told you, I'm not getting the Effect Cube. Don't you understand what happened to Vincent?"

"Charlie, Vincent was an anomaly. The chances of that happening are one in a million. Besides, what happened to

Vincent might have been for the best, at least for you. He was a bad influence. I mean, look at you, considering not getting the Effect Cube! I know Vincent put that idea in your head. He clearly had serious problems."

"You don't know anything about Vincent or about me! I keep telling you, but you don't listen. So fuck off!" I jerk Willow out the door and slam it behind me.

The air is crisp and cool. My head pulses. My dad is like everyone else. Vincent was *too* different. People say, *be unique. Be yourself.* But they don't mean it. It's only okay to be unique up to a point. Beyond that, you've hit Effect Cube territory.

Why am I the only one—now that Vincent is gone—who understands that they can't just Effect-Cube-away everything?

Willow turns toward the shed, barking ferociously.

"Willow, what's wrong?" She's usually such a gentle creature. Of course she is. The Effect Cube Manufacturing and Placement Center—or ECMPC—ensures that everyone in Deali, including the engineered pets, is gentle. Peaceful. *Easy.*

Willow drags me to the shed, her teeth bared. I've never seen this behavior before.

"Okay, Willow. If there's something bothering you this much, let's check it out."

I swing the shed door open. Inside, a young woman is curled into a ball. She doesn't look that much older than me. Her dark brown eyes catch me off guard. Staring. Piercing.

"Please don't hurt me!" the woman cries. Her expression is not one often seen here. It's an expression of fear, and I've really only ever seen it in the programs I watch on the wall screen. Except that one time, as Vincent ducked into the car on that last day. My stomach flops.

"What are you doing in my shed?"

The young woman presses herself further into the corner.

I step closer. Willow leans into my leg. "Are you okay?" I ask.

The ECMPC makes sure everyone has a home and their needs met, so why would this woman be hiding in my shed?

"Please... Just don't hurt me!" The young woman brings her hands to her face. Her skin is hardened and caked with dirt.

"Calm down! I'm not going to hurt you. Who are you afraid is going to hurt you? What's your name? Are you from Deali?" It's too many questions, I realize too late. But I've never seen anyone who was really afraid of another person.

She shakes her head. I can't tell if it's a *yes* or a *no* or which question she's answering, but dust flies everywhere. "Please just don't let the monsters find me!"

Then I notice her neck. She has the circle tattoo that marks someone from the Outlier Zone.

I've got to be the first person who's ever seen someone in Deali with that tattoo. People who go to the Outlier Zone don't come back. Unless of course, they change their minds and agree to get the Effect Cube. But their memories of their time in the O-Z are erased along with their tattoo, so the handful of people who have come back never share anything about what happened when they were away.

"You're from the O-Z. What happened to you?"

"The monsters, they aren't just propaganda! They're real! When I chose to go there instead of getting the Effect

97

Cube… I just assumed it was all a big story. But it's not…"
Her voice breaks. "Can I have some water please? And
maybe some food?"

The thought of being without food or water is
unimaginable. Maybe even more horrific than the existence
of monsters. "Of course. I'll come right back with water and
a meal. Stay here. No one will bother you here, I promise."

I close the shed door carefully and shudder. This
changes everything.

* * *

Willow and I walk through the back door in shock. Not
only did I just meet an Outlier in my backyard shed, but
there's also an ECMPC technician sitting across from my
dad in an armchair in my living room.

"Ah! There you are, Charlotte. We were just talking
about you." My dad's voice is uncomfortable, the one he
uses when he's talking to authority figures. It's forced and
artificial. I hate that voice.

I detour to the kitchen, making each step take far longer
than it should. "Just need to get a glass of water and then I'll
be right over," I say as politely as I can. I settle Willow in
her bed and take my time drinking. Guilt washes over me.
The thirsty, hungry woman is still sitting in my shed.

I finally get to the living room and take the seat as far
away from the technician as possible. His name badge says
Cal.

"Good morning, Charlotte. My name is Technician Cal.
I'm here to talk about your Effect Cube placement,
scheduled in two days."

98

I don't say anything because all I can think of is the woman in the shed and the tiny bit of her story I know and the flashes of Vincent right before he left for his Effect Cube placement and how much I miss him and how weird all of this is. And I know whatever comes out of my mouth is not going to be the right thing. It never is.

Cal stares at me, waiting.

My dad breaks the awkward silence. "So, Technician Cal, as I mentioned, Charlotte is struggling—just a bit—with the idea of the Effect Cube placement because of what happened to her friend, Vincent Isler. Is there anything you can share with Charlotte to help her feel more at ease with this process?"

"Well, of course, Mr. Gale. So, as you both already know, Charlotte's Effect Cube will be polishing her... communication edges." He half smiles and thumbs through his papers. "It has been noted in Charlotte's record that she sometimes struggles to fully listen to teachers and fellow students, and her responses are..." He pauses. "Her responses are not always—*expected*."

This is not new information for me. It's the same report I've received every year.

"In addition, a few of Charlotte's early-grade teachers reported that she talked frequently about 'seeing people's colors.' We aren't sure what that means, and she stopped this behavior around age eleven, but it's something we can easily take care of with the Effect Cube."

My fingers tingle. My heart races. Dad's skin suddenly ripples with pale green, and Technician Cal's rigid face is now a very light blue. I stare at my own hand: flaming orange.

99

Memories of my first day of school flash through my brain. So many new children, so many fun colors. My hands would burn and my heart would beat faster and faster and then *BOOM!* I could see all the colors hiding beneath the boring handful of skin tones in the room. The teacher, of course, was a pale teal. But the class's children were mostly bright red, golden, and purple.

That's when I first met Vincent—the only other orange kid in our room.

Over the years, most children turned light blue or pale green. A few stayed their original color. At least, until the Effect Cube. Over eighteen, *everyone* is a muted shade of green or blue. And by age eleven, I learned that talking about what I could see did not go over well with all those pale-cool-color people.

"Charlotte."

I jump back to the living room. The Colors are gone.

"Charlotte, I can assure you that your Effect Cube is nothing like what Vincent received. Your personality does not need as much refining as his did. And what happened with Vincent is an anomaly. Statistically speaking, hollowing happens less than 0.01% of the time. You can come for your placement procedure completely at ease."

I think carefully about my question before letting out the words. "Technician Cal, if someone doesn't want to get the Effect Cube, what happens in the Outlier Zone?"

"Statistically speaking, Charlotte, as you already know from mathematics in school, about 68 percent of the population of Deali falls within the acceptable range of the Behavior Bell Curve. This means that 32 percent require an

Effect Cube. And it's only a miniscule percentage of people who elect not to get it."

Technician Cal clears his throat. I imagine the idea of that makes him ill at ease.

"Outliers are provided basic living conditions in the O-Z. Of course, the Outlier Zone is *not* Deali. It lacks most of our comfortable, engineered enhancements. Life is not nearly as easy. Many Outliers do choose to return and have the Effect Cube placement. We help their re-entry by erasing their memories of that unpleasant time."

Technician Cal checks his time device and places his papers in his bag. I guess the meeting is over.

"We look forward to seeing you at the ECMPC in two days, Charlotte. We're so excited for you to start this next step of your journey in life. Turning eighteen and getting the Effect Cube is a huge milestone. Mr. Gale, please bring Charlotte and all the necessary papers I gave you when you drop her off."

"Of course, Technician Cal. We're so excited for Charlotte to achieve this important next step."

Technician Cal walks out of the living room, leaving behind a faint imprint of his butt in the armchair seat and a light smell of the lemon soap that's been popular for at least three years. Vincent and I always rolled our eyes as teachers walked by, lemon wafting in every direction.

If we hadn't been one year apart in age, we could have taken our orange selves to the Outlier Zone together. But that's not how it works in Deali. In Deali, you turn eighteen and you have to decide. And Vincent's parents refused to let him go to the O-Z. So much for free will.

Now I have to figure it out on my own.

* * *

Watching from the window, I wait for Technician Cal's car to make the last turn and drive out of sight. Dad is changing into jogging clothes. Perfect. I can finally get back to the shed.

I grab a canteen of water, a box of Nutritional Combo Number Three, and a packet of Nutritional Enjoyment Flavor Number Six—what my great-grandfather says was modelled after the flavor of something called pizza. I slip out to the shed, hoping the woman is still there.

I close the door behind me. The light is dim, but there's a window in the shed, so I can see her huddled in the same corner.

"Here's some food and water." I place everything at her feet and back away to my own corner. It smells rotten—like compost—and it takes me several minutes to understand that it's the woman across from me who's giving off that odor.

"Can you tell me your name?" It might not be the best question to lead with, but I've learned that asking people's names is an expected form of interaction.

"Alice."

That's all she says. I wait only a minute or two for her to devour the food and chug the water. I pull my knees up to my chest so I can bury my nose in the lilac-smell of my pants.

I don't have to ask her any questions. She finishes eating and launches into her story.

"It was *unimaginable*. They take you there on a bus. In my year, no one else chose to go. Everyone who was required to, got the Effect Cube. So I was totally alone.

"They put me in a building they said I could claim, but the walls were wet and cracked and the roof was missing in places. There is no electricity in the O-Z. And no running water. A giant, grotesque creature I later learned was called a rat scurried up and bit my shoe. Five minutes after they dumped me there, I ran out of that place, hoping the bus would still be there waiting for me. But it was gone.

"My building had enough food for one week. After that was gone, I had to venture into other parts of the O-Z. And at first, I couldn't wait to meet other Outliers. I assumed we would all help each other. After all, we had something very important in common. But each person I met was crueler than the last. The longer you live out there, the less *you* you become."

Alice's words stab me in my very core. How could Deali create an alternative world like this and then actually dump people there? Sure, there were rumors about monsters in the O-Z. But all of us just assumed they were stories made up to scare the few doubters into deciding the Effect Cube truly was the best choice.

My voice shakes. "What happened to you? How did you get back?"

Alice stares at me vacantly. Her dark brown eyes half closed, and when they open again, her pupils are so big, they're like holes I find myself drowning in.

"What's your name?" Her question pulls me back to the shed.

"Charlie." I have no other words.

103

"Charlie, the Outlier Zone is not a place for humans to live. The monsters are worse than any story you've ever heard. I barely existed for… I'm not sure how long. There was no way to track days…or even hours. I don't want to tell you what else happened to me. Imagine your worst nightmare, and it's probably true."

"How did you get out?"

The woman across from me closes her eyes and leans into the shed wall. "I ran. I ran for a long time."

I know not to ask any more questions. Instead, *my* story tumbles out. Or maybe it's really Vincent's story. I share about my best friend, his captivating stories, his insights into life, and his quirky sense of humor that always kept me laughing. Tears trickle down my cheek as I tell her about our plans and how it all fell apart.

I don't know if she's listening. Her eyes are closed and she doesn't move.

"The Technician was just here, Alice. They expect me in two days. I don't know what to do."

Moving only her lips, Alice whispers, "Don't make the mistake I did, Charlie."

I stand to leave. I can't be in this shed any longer. "I'll let you rest, and I promise I'll bring more food and water later. Then we can make a plan for you."

Alice is still. I stare. The feeling starts—my fingers tingle and my heart races. The blood drains from my brain. In a brief second, I'll be able to see her Colors. But what I can't understand is when they appear, Alice is very pale blue.

* * *

The birds outside my window sing, but I'm sweaty and cold. Again. For a split second I imagine Vincent there in my room. Orange fading away. Then he's gone. Again.

The concrete steps are cold, but I rush to the kitchen. Dad's running shoes are not in their usual spot. Good. He's already gone jogging. Willow stretches, steps out of her bed, and greets me with a lick.

"You'll have to wait, Willow. Stay here. I'll be back for our walk, but I've got to get some food and water to Alice first."

I fill a canteen with water, grab Nutritional Combo Number Two and Nutritional Enjoyment Flavor Number Two. It's not the best pairing, but it's what's at the front of the cooling cabinet. Then I grab a change of clothes from the basket I didn't feel like putting away the previous evening.

Arms full of supplies for Alice, I hustle to the shed. The shed shudders. I stop. A scratching sound prickles my skin. A low moan and a cough rattle the air. I pull the shed door open slowly.

Alice isn't there. Instead, a strange abomination sits in her place. Its limbs are long and muscular, the body elongated. The skin is pale gray and leathery. But the head is Alice's. The dark brown eyes remain.

I drop everything. For a moment, I can't move.

But the creature can.

It reaches its hideous arms toward me. I slam the shed door.

"Charlie, please…"

"Alice, is that you?" My throat clenches. My stomach squirms.

"Yes, Charlie. Help me…"

Alice's voice stabs me in the heart. I open the shed door, but I don't dare to go inside. "What happened, Alice?"

Alice's pupils dilate until each whole eye is black. She smiles but it's all pain. "I was in the Outlier Zone too long. I told you the monsters were real. What I didn't tell you is that it's the Outliers who become the monsters."

I drop down in the doorway of the shed.

"At first, I saw only humans and monsters. And of course, every human Outlier is terrified of the monsters lurking in the O-Z because we all saw what they were capable of. I never understood that eventually *every* Outlier would transform into one."

"I don't understand. What are you talking about?"

"I assume it was a few months in. The group I had become part of started complaining of pain. In a matter of days, their arms and legs grew longer, their skin changed, and finally..." She stops. Her eyes plead with me. "And finally, this. Well, almost. I'm not there yet."

"But... how? How does this happen? You're all humans. Do they do something to you?"

"I joined one more group after that. They all had seen the same thing. Someone said there must be something in the Outlier Zone—that the Deali engineers must have created a world that would wind up like that. I don't know. But whether they engineered it on purpose or it has something to do with the environment there, that's the outcome: Outliers turn into monsters."

Every vein in Alice's body bulges. She clutches at her head. Claws rip through her fingertips. Blood flows down her pale gray arms. She lurches forward onto her feet.

I leap to mine, ready to run back to the house.

106

"I hoped I had left in time. Oh, Charlie...." She lets loose a roar, head tilted back, body quivering.

I step backward. Alice pushes through the doorway. She stumbles. Then she finds her balance and rushes out.

By the time I can move and sprint to the road, Alice is almost out of view.

I don't have the heart to notify anyone. And even if I did, I wouldn't be able to find the words to tell the story. I pick up the clothing and food I dropped and shuffle back to the house. I climb the concrete steps back to my room.

It's still morning, but I crawl into bed. And even though I can't sleep, I have no problem staying there all day.

* * *

"Charlie, are you awake? Today's the day!"

I'm cold and sweaty, like every morning for the last year. But my nightmares of Vincent are further away today.

My bare feet tingle on the concrete steps, and Willow licks them as I emerge into the kitchen. Dad has gone all out: Nutritional Combo Number Twenty *and* Nutritional Enjoyment Flavor Number Eight wait at my seat. We can almost never get those. It's a treat my great-grandfather says reminds him of something called waffles with butter and maple syrup.

"I'm so proud of you, Charlie. Eat up. We have to leave in an hour." He jogs out the door.

The car ride is quick. Dad drones on about the party he's planned for the evening. "Music... Don't you think?... Nutritional Flavor Three for the drinks?... Have to send everyone home by midnight, of course...."

107

I only catch bits of what he says. My mind swirls with images of Alice, though it's Vincent's words that linger in my ears. That last conversation I can never forget.

"It's okay, Charlie."

"No, it's not, Vincent. You're going to be different."

"Actually, I think that's what they're working to correct, right?"

I can't laugh. *"You know what I mean."*

"Let's just see what happens. Ultimately, it'll still be me."

"Are you sure?"

"Pretty sure."

He reaches for my hand. My fingers tingle. My heart races. I love watching the burnt orange of my fingers entwined with the rust orange of Vincent's. Until his parents yell that it's time to leave...

"Here we are, Charlie." Dad pulls up to the ECMPC. Technician Cal is standing at the door with a nurse.

"Welcome, Charlotte. We're so glad you're here. Nurse Amity will take you to your room. Mr. Gale, everything should be wrapped up in two hours. You can wait here or come back then."

"What would you prefer, Charlie? Would you like me to wait here for you?"

"Sure, Dad. That would be nice."

He hugs me. It's the first time in years.

Nurse Amity chatters as we walk down the brightly lit corridor. The ECMPC looks like a hotel. The floor is carpeted, and the walls are covered in thick, floral wallpaper. She opens a door. I expect something like a hospital room, but instead it really is just like a hotel.

108

"You can have a seat on the bed, Charlotte."

I smooth the bedspread, tracing the flowers.

Nurse Amity walks over with a tray. Several small cups wait for me.

"Okay, Charlotte. Once you drink these medications, you'll become very sleepy. You'll lie here for a little while, then we'll take you to the Placement Room. After the Effect Cube is inserted and tested, we'll bring you back here. And after about half an hour, you can go home with your dad. Sound good?"

I nod. How do I explain that none of this really ever sounded good? But here I am. I drink the medicine in each of the cups.

I know I'll be asleep in a matter of seconds. I lie back on the pillows. It can't be real, but I'm convinced I see Vincent, sitting at the small table for two in the corner of the room.

Nurse Amity leans down. "How do you feel, Charlotte?"

"I feel…different."

* * *

Charlotte's dad greets her with a hug, "How do you feel, Dear?"

Charlotte smiles. "I'm fine, Dad. I don't remember a thing." She takes his arm.

"Wonderful! Wonderful! I've completed all the paperwork with Technician Cal, so we can head home and get ready for your party."

"That's great, Dad."

Charlotte holds her hand out. She wiggles her fingers. She studies how they move. It's a compelling urge she cannot control, but she has no idea why she does it. She thinks she's supposed to see something, something that isn't really there. But it's just a hand. It's the last time she does this.

The new Effect Cube recipient and her father exit the ECMPC, passing a group of technicians at the front of the building. Charlotte makes eye contact with a young female technician. The woman's dark brown eyes draw Charlotte in with their piercing gaze.

"Did everything go well, Charlotte?" the technician asks.

Charlotte stares at the woman's name tag: *Alice*.

"Yes, everything went very well, Technician Alice. Thank you." Charlotte pauses. She knows she has said exactly what she's supposed to, but she can't shake the feeling she needs to ask an additional question. "Is there any possibility I know you from somewhere?"

"I believe we might have met once. But I do get that a lot. I'm so glad everything was easy and you're ready for this next important step in life." Technician Alice holds the door open for Charlotte and her dad.

Charlotte laughs throughout the entire party. She dances and sips the delicious drinks her dad splurged to provide. As expected, everyone leaves at midnight. Charlotte waves goodbye and still has the energy to clean up the kitchen before heading to bed.

She wakes the next morning, warm and comfortable. Sitting on the edge of her bed, the flash of a dream darts through her mind. She's holding hands with someone. A boy. She can't remember his name.

Charlotte heads down to the kitchen. Her dad calls out to her from the front door, "Charlotte, I'm headed out for my jog. It's nice to see you up so early."

"Have a good run, Dad. I'll leave some breakfast out for you."

Willow greets her with a lick and a few pleading cries for a walk. Charlotte finds the leash and the two head outside. In the bright morning sun, the dream returns. It's a momentary burst of memory. She's watching the sunset with the boy, red and yellow and orange falling to the horizon, the sky becoming a lovely shade of light blue. And she smiles.

Justice

by
Ali Bryant

I once learned in science class that all the cells in our bodies are replaced every seven years. How lovely it is to know that one day I will have a body *He* never touched.

How lovely it would be to actually sleep instead of jolting awake with night terrors—which always leave me sitting for hours with my knees drawn to my chest worrying where *He* is. *He* could be anywhere and that scares me...but what terrifies me is that he might come back to the school. I hope they don't let that happen. Then again, they really don't care as much as they should.

More than anything, how lovely it would be to not worry about what I'll hear when I arrive at the toxic whirlpool that is Greenbay Charter, swirling and conspiring to pull me under.

All survivors can hope for when they come forward is to be supported, understood, and encouraged.

Instead, we hear the diminishing words:

It was just a little fun.
It's your word against his.
What were you wearing?
Why didn't you fight back harder?
Why did you wait so long to report it?
I'd believe him over you any day.
This will ruin his life.
It could have been worse.
It's been long enough. Get over it.
You won't heal if you keep talking about it.
Prove it.

Slut.

Exaggerating.

Your own fault.

Isn't it fascinating how words are so simple yet can hold so much power? When you think about it, the act of speaking really is the simplest task of them all; we open our mouths, let noise rumble from our vocal cords, and move our tongues to shape and sound things out. It's so simple, so easy, people do it without even thinking of what they're saying. They do it carelessly, cruelly, without another thought, as if the words cease to exist once they leave the speaker's lips. Words can lift us up or tear us down. With words, a war can be brought or a peace brokered. With words, a heart can be healed or torn beyond repair. With words, inspiration can be sparked or self-esteem shattered and trodden into the ground. Words are medicine and weapons; they unite and divide.

Even something as common as *I'm fine, how are you?*

As I sit before my mirror, lit up with white lights and basking my tear-streaked cheeks within the glow, words are not simple nor powerful to my tongue. They are difficult, weak, *painful*. Each word I speak to myself betrays my emotions. Practiced phrases feel shallow, hollow, a lie. Yet, I continue to stare myself in the eyes, a fake smile etched across my face as freshly applied mascara leaves a wet trail on my cheeks.

I hunt for good words, excellent words. I reach deep into the word barrel and stir piles of rotting words, barely alive. Sometimes, fine words come easily, but not so today. *Where are all the healing words when we need them?* The dark ones buzz in the barrel like bees and tempt me to give up. I am unsure and tremble. I pity myself. A panic grips me. No good words appear. So, I settle for the ones I have:

"I'm fine."

113

I repeat them over and over until they feel generic, dull, more fake and less truthful than before. My face hurts as I force my smile further, bearing my teeth and squinting as my eyes pool with fresh tears.

"I'm fine."

It's better to betray my feelings than to be open about them. No one cares how I feel, even though they pretend to. They fake it and so do I. In practice of how I will speak to everyone today, I'm so bold as to add room for a response, giving them a chance to follow the script.

"How are you?"

Their answers will all be the same.

I'm good.

I'm doing great.

I'm fine as well.

No one just randomly opens up to a person and spits out the truth, because what are they supposed to say?

Oh, I feel like shit, but that's ok!

Sometimes, we might feel inclined to. We might feel a want so heavy it threatens to tear through our throats, but we don't let it out. And it's better that way. It's better to pretend that the world is *fine* rather than acknowledge the reality that it's turned to shit.

And so, through my silent cries, through the tears running down my cheeks, through the mascara leaving yet another dark streak in its wake, through the pain throbbing in my face from smiling so big and for so long, through the pitiful emotions I *actually* feel...I speak the simplest words that have a crueler power than any others:

"I'm fine, how are you?"

* * *

114

"I'm fine, how are you?"

Rain patters against the window overlooking the yard from the school social worker's office where I attend weekly meetings to assess my mental health. How fun.

"I'm good. So, where did we leave off last week…"

Ms. Hartley. She's one of the only people in this place I'm actually fond of. She may wear her grey hair in a beehive style that is completely out of date, and she may have a mole on her face that *must* weigh a pound and a half, but her good intentions are what I admire.

I shrug in response to her question. I never really talk in these sessions that much.

She sighs. "Have you slept at all since I last saw you?" Her voice is soft and sympathetic as she takes in my appearance. I guess the makeup didn't help as much as I thought it would. Is concealer more to hide blemishes or feelings?

Again, I use gestures to answer her, shaking my head *no*.

"Ali…You need to take better care of yourself. Not sleeping and not talking won't solve anything. What about your room?"

I finally look at her.

"Yes, your mom told me about that."

Of course she did.

"Have you started cleaning it yet?"

This is different from the typical teenager who doesn't want to clean her room scenario. My room is trashed, and honestly, I did it to myself. None of my clothes are put away, clean mixed with the dirty. Paper plates, dishes, and abandoned food are littered upon my desk and dresser, probably attracting bugs…but I can't find the energy to care or do anything about it. *Depression is a bitch.* It sucks the

115

energy and willpower right out from under you until there's nothing left but lazy emptiness and the feeling that you don't deserve nice things.

I hang my head in shame.

Before Ms. Hartley can say anything, three harsh knocks sound at the door. I jump in surprise and she places a hand on my knee to relax me, but I only shy away from her and shrink into myself.

Do not touch me.

She notices my stiffened posture and retracts her hand.

"I almost forgot, Principal Adeline requested to join our session today to discuss something with you. Is that alright?"

As if I wasn't already frozen enough, now I'm a damn statue.

Not her. Not one of them. She doesn't care enough. The words threaten to leave me, but no sound comes from my mouth. Nothing ever does. Nothing comes easily. So, I simply nod my head again, not having any fight in me.

Ms. Hartley stands to open the door for Principal Adeline, and as she steps in, my palms dampen with sweat. The top of my head burns as the rest of me flushes. A heavy ball of dread forms in the pit of my stomach. Something bad is about to happen.

"Hello, Ali."

The couch dips as she sits next to me and the hairs on the back of my neck stand. She pushes her boy-cut hair off her forehead then smooths any creases in her blazer. Her thick-rimmed glasses are adjusted on her nose before she turns to look at me. I avoid eye-contact.

"I came to let you know how we are handling the situation with the student you reported."

My silence gives her the okay to continue.

"His suspension is ending today, and he'll be returning after the weekend is over."

All the air leaves my lungs. Bile rises in my throat. I don't think my heart has ever beat this fast.

"I do not want you to worry because we will be taking strict safety precautions. He will be supervised by a teacher at all times. We made sure you will not see him in any of your classes..."

This can't be possible. This can't be real. Surely they wouldn't let him back after what he did. Maybe I'm having another night terror?

"I just want to do whatever I can to make you feel safe."

That's when something in me snaps.

I shock even myself as I stand up and tower over her sitting form. "If you wanted to keep me safe then you wouldn't let him come back to the fucking school!"

"Ali, calm down," Ms. Hartley tells me, but I ignore her.

"He assaulted me. He assaulted Lily. He threatened to *kill* us. We are *minors.* He is eighteen. He doesn't have to be here! Why wouldn't you expel him? Why would you let him come back? What the hell is wrong with you?"

"Ali. Sit down now." Principal Adeline points to the couch.

I slowly lower myself, but my newfound rage does not diminish.

"I understand your frustration—"

"Understand? If you understood how I felt, then you wouldn't be doing this. He won't give a damn about your safety precautions. He's not someone who lets rules or the word 'no' stop him from getting what he wants. Haven't you learned that people who act like they have nothing to lose are the most dangerous?"

"Ali, please let me finish."

117

I grit my teeth.

"I *do* understand your frustration, but there is nothing more we can do here. We are not allowed to expel students."

That doesn't make any sense. Greenbay is a charter school, not public. They accept people who choose to come here based on their academic capabilities, finance, and chance in the lottery, whereas public schools are forced to take anyone unless the student faces criminal circumstances. People come and go here as they please. Students can be expelled, but as usual, they continue to lie.

"Aren't you legally obligated to report sexual abuse within the school? Why haven't you gotten the police involved? More than one student came forward and you're just gonna sit back and watch as things get worse?"

"It's more difficult than you think. We don't have parental consent from Lily—"

"So get it! You know she's afraid to go to the police on her own. Have you even tried to do something? You aren't protecting us!"

"Well, I'm afraid that if you want anything more done you will have to do it yourself. Alone. File a report, but I don't think it will get you very far."

Frustrated tears threaten to spill but I blink them back.

"I *am* on your side you know."

That's funny. I know she is nowhere near my side. I'm not supposed to do this on my own. It shouldn't be left up to me simply because they failed to report a crime for the sake of their own reputation. Everywhere you look there are banners hanging and messages posted on *FaceBook*, all claiming that Greenbay Charter is a school of opportunity and the best education. Why wouldn't they try to save themselves?

118

I refuse to let their reputation win. I *will* take matters into my own hands.

* * *

I've never been in such a small room before. The only source of light is a desk lamp radiating white heat from the middle of a round table where I sit, making things seem even more claustrophobic. My mother is a chair away, clutching her handbag tightly on her lap. My knee bounces up and down. A fingernail is lodged between my teeth as I chew on it. Sweat beads on my forehead. Why is that lamp so hot? What is taking so long? A clock hangs on the wall and my heart speeds up with every tick growing louder than the last.

Tick-tock. I'm starting to regret coming here. *Tick-TOCK.* Maybe this wasn't the best idea. *TICK-TOCK.* I should go home...

The door swings open. Sheriff Collins walks through...but my gaze shifts to the officer behind him who I'm guessing is supposed to take my statement.

The *male* officer.

I'm about to share the personal and grotesque details of what led me here to a *man*.

My discomfort does not go unnoticed as the Sheriff speaks up. "I know you probably wanted a woman, but Winston here is the only one on duty. I'm sorry." His voice is kind. "I'm gonna step out of the room and let him take over. Got this, Winston?"

He nods and makes his way to the table. A stack of papers plop on the surface before he sits down. He's quite young.

"Hi, Ali. I wish we could've met under better circumstances, but it is nice to meet you."

119

I muster the best smile I can manage.

"Basically, how this works is you need to be prepared to give real, honest information to questions I ask. What you tell me you will write afterward in a statement; you can have as much paper as you'd like. The form will ask for your name, address, and social security number. Recount events in as much detail as possible. Think of the who/what/when /where/why/how of the incident. Also, remember that you are making an official statement and that filing a false police report is a crime."

I nod, overwhelmed.

"Okay. First question. What is the name of the student who assaulted you?"

I tell him.

"Next question. When and where did the incident take place?"

"There was more than one incident that happened through September, but they all took place at the school."

"Can you try to remember the exact dates?"

"I—I have no idea. Sorry. Wait. The last one was just a couple of weeks ago on a Thursday, I think."

My mom pulls the pocket calendar from her handbag and flips through the pages. "Thursday two weeks ago was September 26th."

"Perfect," the officer replies. "And that's the only specific date you can remember?"

"Yeah, sorry."

"That's okay. Are there any names you can list of people who may be aware of his behavior, who could've seen the things he's done?"

I name people ranging from friends, to acquaintances who've talked about him, to people I've hardly spoken to but

120

have seen the way he's acted with them. Lily is one of the people on the list.

"We actually talked to Lily not that long ago. She made a statement but refused to press charges. The poor girl was shaking the whole time. I think she was terrified of going against him."

"She's not terrified of going against him, she's terrified *of* him. We all are. He's not someone that lets you walk away from him." I know. I'm her best friend. This was something we went through together.

"I'm aware of that. As a matter of fact, we have an ongoing case with this guy. His history isn't exactly the best. He got expelled from his public school last year for something similar to what he's done to you. Girl pressed charges, but since he was still a minor, he got off with probation and a court-order to attend Greenbay."

Court-order? A million things fly through my mind. *Who was this girl? Is she okay now? I almost gave my trust to someone who's a serial offender?* My most prominent thought is: *The school already knew about his behavior but waited until now to think about safety precautions?* They might have been able to prevent this but didn't even try. They weren't protecting us from the start.

"But hey," Winston pulls my attention back, "Guess what?"

"What?"

A smile breaks out across his face. "September 26th was two weeks after he turned eighteen. He can be charged as an adult. We're gonna get this guy. He shouldn't get to roam free after the pain he's caused you and other girls."

His confidence soothes me, and compassion is something I've longed for since the lack thereof at Greenbay. But this feeling of comfort does not last long.

"Back to the questions. These... may be uncomfortable."

"Okay..."

"I need to know where he touched you."

Oh.

"You don't have to say anything. We have a chart you can mark-up instead." He places a diagram of a woman's anatomy in front of me. Each of her body parts are labeled with a check-mark box next to it.

"Just put a check wherever he's touched you." He hands me a pen and I take it with trembling hands.

I don't think anyone ever expects to be in this situation, but here I am. I guess it happens to those who least expect it...and those who are most vulnerable.

Mouth. Check.

Neck. Check

Breasts. Check.

Abdomen. Check

Hips. Check.

Buttocks. Check.

Thighs. Check.

Genitalia. Check.

After marking the boxes like I'm grading a quiz, I hand the sheet back to him, still embarrassed that I'm answering such personal questions to a man.

"Did he penetrate you?"

I freeze. This is so embarrassing. I've never been so humiliated in my entire life. Tears begin to well again as I turn red. Still, I respond with the shake of my head.

"Okay, Ali. Last thing you have to do for us is fill out the report, then you are free to go home."

I take a deep breath, summoning the strength and composure for this final stretch.

"I'll be talking to the Sheriff outside while you do that. Take all the time and paper that you need." He leaves the room.

As soon as the door closes, I reach over to hold my mother's hand and give it a comforting squeeze. "Mom," I cry. That one word means so much between us. A cry for help. A want for her to save me. But, more than anything, an apology. I know how tough this must be on her.

Despite the tears in her eyes, the smile she gives me is warm and reassuring. "It's not your fault, Miss. Now go on. Think of it like a book and write it out like you always do. I'm here." She squeezes my hand a final time before letting go.

I pick up the pen again and take one of the sheets from beside me, then begin writing. Telling stories was something I always loved doing; boxes in the basement are filled with scribbles and illustrations on pages from years that have come and gone. I always felt as if I were preparing to write a big story someday. I just never knew this would be it.

Words that say *He held me in place...He pushed his tongue inside my mouth...His hands slid down...*fly across the page like antic shapes in dreams. And, by the time it's all over, I'm exhausted.

Just as we're on our way out, Sheriff Collins calls behind us. "Oh, and don't worry, we'll make sure he doesn't set foot on campus anytime soon."

I smile in gratitude and wave him goodbye.

Outside, night has fallen and the blue haze of the day lifted itself to reveal stars. Nights when I can't sleep, and even now as I take in the glistening sky, I always wonder if we were nocturnal, would we feel more connected to those far away stars? Perhaps, sensing the fragility of Earth all the more? To me, the night sky is when the curtain is pulled

123

back, when we get to look out the window we call the sky and into the universe beyond. I dream that whatever lies beyond is full of peace and equality, and hopefully someday I'll get there. It isn't always so bad not being able to sleep...the dreams I have awake are so much better.

Our car doors shutting is the only sound that can be heard echoing in the nearly empty parking lot. Neither of us say anything at first, taking a moment to catch our breaths and process everything that just happened.

My mother breaks the silence first, trying to phrase whatever was spinning within her fraught mind. "Y'know...when you were born, I told your father that 'this will be a whole other ballpark.' I'm sure he didn't understand what I meant—he never really did in our fourteen years of marriage—but I knew, looking down at you, seeing this innocent, precious little girl in my arms, that I would need to protect you from the dangers of the world. I was protective of your brother too, don't get me wrong, but...being a woman and giving birth to a woman after witnessing the way that we are preyed upon...I just went into full mama bear mode."

I laugh at the last part despite my watering eyes.

"You always used to get mad at me for worrying about every little thing, but now do you understand why I worried so much? I never wanted you to be subjected to this kind of situation. I spent the entirety of your fifteen years on this planet praying and doing whatever I could to prevent it. But here we are." Her voice drops to a whisper, as if she's trying to let it sink in. "We just sat in a room together while you described the way a man had violated you."

"Mom, I'm so, so sorry."

Her voice is gentle yet stern all at once as she speaks. "No. No, Ali. You do not get to be sorry for anything. None of what happened is your fault. Every piece of blame falls on him. The only other person who should be sorry is me. I'm sorry that I failed you."

"You didn't! There was nothing you could've done. No matter how hard you try to protect someone they will always get hurt in the end. It's inevitable. It's the world. If it didn't happen now it would've happened at some point, and that's the sad truth."

"Yeah, it is."

Another beat of silence.

"Am I still your daughter?" My voice is barely audible.

I feel her hand under my chin as she turns me to face her. I'm forced to look her in the eyes for the first time since we've sat in the car, and I see that they are tear-filled like mine.

"Why would you even ask such a thing? Of course you're my daughter. Nothing will ever change that. Despite all of this, you are still you." She brushes my messy hair back with her other hand so she can see my face better. A small smile tugs at the corners of her lips. "You're my little Miss Munch."

My heart warms at the familiar nickname. "Sometimes, I just don't feel like myself anymore, you know? I feel less human. Like a...like a—"

"Like an object. Yeah, that's how it feels after we're violated. Like something has been taken away from us. Like we've been used."

She said it better than I could.

"But you'll feel whole again. I know you will because you're strong. You did something big today. Give yourself credit for it." She leans in to kiss my forehead.

"You're one step closer to getting Justice."

125

* * *

Ten Months Later

* * *

Six years, one month, nine days, ten hours, twenty-three minutes, sixteen seconds.

That's how long it is until I'll have a body he never touched.

I've only seen him once since that night, and when I did it wasn't as frightening as I thought it would be. Every night terror prepared me for the worst. Seeing him was never the scariest part of the dream, neither was the bloodbath or manipulation that would subsequently occur, it was always the feeling leading up to it. This dreadful, heavy sense that my dreams were shifting south. In reality, the moment I saw him was abrupt. I had no idea he would be at the school that day. There was no sixth-sense. I just turned a corner and BOOM! There he was, standing in the lobby, waiting to be called into Adeline's office with his father and an officer at his side. I later found out it was for an investigatory meeting that would be crucial to the second-degree charges I pressed against him.

I saw him first, but it was only seconds later that those eyes, those ice-cold eyes I still see in the heads of other people met mine, and for a moment I was brought back to that lonely table sitting behind Building #3, with forgotten, overgrown grass tangling up its legs.

"I love you."

"I'll never hurt you."

His hands grope me. I do not want them.

"Don't cry."

His lips graze my skin. I do not want them.

"Maybe you shouldn't have worn those leggings."

"You were begging me for it."

His words...diminishing words...tear down my self-worth. I do not want them.

So, I fought them. So, I still fight them.

The table is just that—a table. And *He* is just a man. A person. A pitiful excuse for human life.

An idiot who seemed to believe he could shoot eye-lasers like Superman somewhere in that small mind.

Small.

He once seemed like a giant to me. I feared him. I feared that he could crush me under his gaze at any time. But, as he continued to glare at me, there was a brief, fleeting moment when I realized that *He* is not what haunts me. He has no power over me. he is small.

What haunts me is the violation. What haunts me is that the choice was ripped from my grasp.

In those moments, I wasn't a human being to him. I was an object. I had no voice.

Take a minute and imagine that you have no voice. Subject yourself to a situation where you wish you could scream for help but no one will hear you. Maybe you're trapped in a fire and your voice doesn't carry over the sirens outside. Maybe you're drowning. Maybe a hand is wrapped around your neck and a tongue is down your throat, silencing you of anything you have to say. Terrifying isn't it? Being in a place where your voice can't save you?

It's enough to cause night terrors.

After this revelation, he shrunk. His effect on me shrunk. Instead of coiling away or shrinking into a dismal mentality like I always had, I pushed forward with a power and voice that should've always been in my grasp and stood

127

tall in front of him. The seven small words I uttered put every diminishing word that was once thrown my way to shame.

"You're a lot smaller than I remember."

And then I walked on as if he was never there in the first place.

He. He. he.

But this story isn't about him. And as I write this, I'm realizing more and more that the story isn't about just me either.

This is the story of millions of people around the world.

The story of every one-in-six females who will experience sexual assault.

The story of every one-in-ten males who will experience sexual assault.

The story of a new person every seventy-three seconds in America who has been assaulted.

This is the story of a mother, a father, a daughter, a son, a person of color, a person of the LGBTQ+ community. The story of anyone who has ever been affected by sexual assault. The story of everyone who has been unjustified.

This shouldn't be the story, but it is.

The worst part of it all is feeling alone. It's blaming yourself and feeling less than because you must've been chosen for a reason. It's feeling like you've been singled out in a crowd. Like everyone around you shines brightly, but the grimy hands that touched you left dirt smeared on your skin that taints the light you hold. You second-guess every look in your direction because paranoia tells you they're either judging you, pitying you, or want to hurt you too.

You are not alone. I am not alone, which was something I had discovered very soon.

Greenbay Charter, as I've come to find out, is responsible for sweeping countless offenses under the rug to save the reputation they hold so dearly. And at what cost? The way things were disguised, I never would've guessed it was a place full of secrets and lies, a lot wouldn't have, that's why so many had fallen victim to the horrid nature they continue to hide.

Four years ago, another girl who was a freshman at the time got raped by a senior in the girl's bathroom. She was terrified to go to the police on her own and turned to the school for help. And what did they do? They let him graduate.

She is just one of the very many. I was the final straw.

Suddenly, there were groups of people on my side all fighting in an effort to put this to an end. A friend had gone so far as to organize a walkout stemmed from her Class President campaign gone rouge.

I remember being pushed from the crowd towards the table where she stood, inviting me to join her proudly on top. I remember not wanting to at first because it was *that* table. Diminishing words tried to creep in my head again, but I remembered...a table is just a table. And then I climbed to the top.

Actions speak way the hell louder than words do anyway.

More and more people stood on top of that table, even Lily who held my hand tightly in hers as the color finally started to come back to her beautiful, ebony skin. Suddenly the table had a whole new meaning.

This was now the table where we fought for our Justice.

Hundreds of faces were staring at me, all with expectant looks. A breath of freedom escaped my lips. Welcome to the final show.

A hand grasped mine tighter. The other was soon taken by another. Sweat dripped down the back of my neck. The crowd was still agape. They encouraged me to go further.

A walkout. A protest. A movement. A fight.

The somber mood gave nothing but silence in our honor. Phones were raised high in the air, capturing everything on camera, ready to expose Greenbay Charter to social media. We all had stripped of our uniform jackets in a fleeting moment of freedom, the sea of green churning to rippling waves as they were thrown to the sky before crashing to shore.

There was an instant where I paused and just wondered, *how in the hell did I end up here?*

Everything leading to that moment was blurred by adrenaline, my memory only able to recollect fragments.

Skin on skin.

Diminishing words.

Devastation.

Police stations.

Comfort.

Confessions.

Revelations.

A walkout. A protest. A movement. A fight.

Justice.

We all found a small bit of peace within ourselves that day.

But the story isn't over. The story will never be over as long as hunger and greed are alive.

All we can do is have hope and heal. For some people, healing is hope...it's fighting for what they know is worth having. For others, hope is hopeless. We all heal in our own ways, but the process is the same. Feel it, understand it, overcome it.

130

Writing this is my healing. Writing this is me being the woman I want to be, not the woman diminishing words tell me I should be.

I will never again let a man tell me he loves me as his hands wander where I do not want them. I should be the one making the decisions. I am the one who says yes or no. He was wrong. They are wrong. No isn't yes in disguise. This is a reminder.

The trauma will remain. The trauma will always remain, but as the months continue to go on, his face becomes more and more of a blur.

I pressed charges. Greenbay's student rates have plummeted in all aspects. I transferred schools, and many others have left. I finally cleaned that room.

I've shut the door on *all* my demons of the past.

A new chapter starts now. This story is my goodbye.

This story is my Justice.

Dedication

I would like to thank those who have been there for me through thick and thin, you know who you are, but more than anyone, I'd like to thank my mother who loves and supports me. This story is dedicated not only to her and her good graces, but to all victims of harassment and/or assault. Anyone can be subjected to this cruel behavior; whether you are female, male, black, white, straight, gay, etc. It can happen to anyone. Know that you are not alone, you are not worthless, weak, or objectified. You are strong. You have been through Hell and back, yet you've survived. Consider this story your award, a piece of your story being told, and some measure of *Justice*.

About the Authors

Amber Bliss (Editor) holds an MFA in Writing Popular Fiction from Seton Hill University and an MLIS from the University of Rhode Island. With a combination of creativity, determination, and a little sorcery, she's managed to combine her passion for writing and tabletop RPGs into her work as a librarian. Amber's days are consumed by stories, whether she's writing them, reading them, or telling them around a table cluttered with dice and character sheets because stories don't only make us werewolves and wizards, they make us human. Her own work can be found in *The Monstrous Feminine* by Scary Dairy Press. You can visit Amber at www.amberbliss.com or follow her @am_bliss on Twitter.

Toshiro Brooks is an aspiring author and filmmaker, and lover of horror stories, movies, and games. He lives in Pawtucket, Rhode Island and can be found on Twitter as @BrooksToshiro.

Ali Bryant is a writer, which, considering you are reading this, makes perfect sense. She is best known for her books on Wattpad with an outstanding total of over 32,000 worldwide online readers. She has been thrice nominated for the Red Feather Award, along with one nomination in the historical fiction category for the Wattys 2019. A writer in all genres, she hopes to one day bring her work off the page and onto the screen. Follow her @nostaleo on Wattpad or contact her via email at missalib5314@gmail.com.

Kaia Dahlin lives in Portsmouth, Rhode Island with her family and pets. She found a love of horror in the seventh grade. When she isn't writing, she likes to paint, listen to musicals, and sew, though she promises she doesn't source her own materials.

Kerith Fontenault is an animal-loving human (*currently* human, at least) who enjoys reading, playing RPGs, eating cream doughnuts, and taking long, preferably barefooted, walks near the woods. Sometimes she will wear shoes (probably rain boots), but would much rather stay at home teaching her rat tricks, though she hasn't had any luck with 'speak' yet.

Theresa Katin lives in Portsmouth, Rhode Island with her family. She enjoys writing a variety of speculative fiction and has a soft spot for poetry. In her spare time, she loves to play the clarinet and do karate.

Nathan Moone is a Creative Writing major at Ithaca College with a passion for horror (yes, creepy crawlies included) and the drama that ensues. Nathan's love of travel and exploration starting when he travelled to Australia as a US representative for Track and Field in High School. In his free time, he is an acrobat in a circus and enjoys watching films whenever possible. You can find more of him on Twitter and Instagram at @Moone_Writes.

Linden Philo is a resident story creator and WIP animator who is passionate about social justice and exploring the depth of fiction with anyone who wants to talk about it. He enjoys tacos, Anime, and—when he has to leave the house—wandering in forests. He lives in Rhode Island with his family, including one needy dog and four cuddly cats. He promises there will be more Charlie stories and insists he actually appreciates both orange and blue.

Brianna Timpson lives in Rhode Island with her family and dog, Princess. Her love of writing sparked when she was in second grade. When not putting pen to paper, she loves to swim and do Krav Maga (self-defense for anyone). Follow her on Twitter @BriannaTimpson, Instagram @briannatimpson2020, and Facebook.

CPSIA information can be obtained
at www.ICGtesting.com
Printed in the USA
LVHW052218020222
710069LV00010B/649